Awakening Kyras

Jacob Yastrow

D1571232

Acknowledgments

While many elements within this book are based on real events, the author warrants mindful consideration before replicating or attempting situations described herein after. Readers are encouraged to take a trip into an old growth redwood forest or another pristine ecosystem/landscape accessible to them in their local region. Soil compaction and trampling of plants and similar organic matter can cause significant and irreversible damage. Entire worlds and microcosms exist within leaf litter and pristine soil is an asset as vital as clean air or water with value greater than propane or gold. Please stay on the trails and don't climb on logs or fallen vegetation. Tree climbing has its place, however, consult and work with arborists, botanists and expert climbers before risking your safety and the innumerable diversity of life forms comprising the mosaic of life. These intricate ecosystems are generally magnitudes more complex in an old growth forest or mature grassland than what is often left after people take more than the land can sustain.

The land is a gift that we are unconditionally given. It is our duty to nurture and ensure a long-term sustainable future for precious places which cannot be re-created once destroyed.

If I could, I would give it all to the trees, for I am here because I was enticed and intrigued, enamored with incomparable elation, lost in the moment amidst the peaks, trees, rivers, ocean and fog.

Thanks to the land for inspiration and the vibrantly extraordinary beings who showed me that there was more than my realm of perception.

Thank you to my family, friends and all who hosted me or crossed my path on my nomadic pilgrimage from Colorado to Maine. Most notably, David Mitchell and his wife, Michiko for welcoming me into their food forest. David opened my eyes to new light and Michiko taught me how to weave a basket out of poplar bark.

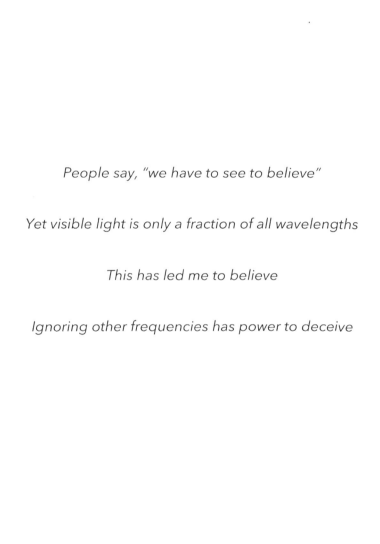

People say, "we have to see to believe"

Yet visible light is only a fraction of all wavelengths

This has led me to believe

Ignoring other frequencies has power to deceive

The Eye Doctor

The optometrist paused and Kyros was clearly irritated.
Lincoln had sped through the examination with little to no
interest in his subject. The last hour was silent aside from
procedural questions asked with indifference, which Kyros
lifelessly answered.

After taking several breaths, the first glimpse of self-
reflection since the start of the appointment, Lincoln's eyes
met Kyros' to humbly apologize for being short and
snappy. "I won't burden you with the details, but this
morning my doctor told me I have cancer. The news
altered my perception. Initially I was filled with fear, but
when I got to work another sensation came over me. The
fright was replaced with dread and regret. It was as if I was

looking through someone else's glasses. My head hurt. I wasn't able to receive what I was given.

"Just now, I'm beginning to see through the blur and understand an alternate truth. Life used to be about work and money, but maybe it's really about something so much greater. Look at this office. I am successful, yet so unfulfilled. I'm beginning to feel a lot like I did something or some things wrong.

"Today, like me, you will see through new lenses. While mine are the product of a diagnosis, yours are the product of a new pair of glasses."

"I'm sorry to hear that." Kyros, a Senior at the local High School, felt the mood shift and attempted a response. Hardly compassionate or empathetic, he could care less about the health of a stranger. The insincere condolences were more of an attempt to accelerate the process.

Lincoln didn't seem to mind the lack of authenticity. "Thanks, but don't worry about me, boy. Just make sure you're not sorry when your time comes."

"What do you mean?" Kyros preferred to not be lectured and came off a little sassy.

The man slowly shook his head side to side and silently said, "Live your best life. You will see... Come, Let's see what we have for frames."

Lincoln increased his volume to an appropriate level and gave Kyros his prescription. The increase in volume seemed odd at first. Kyros reflected that Lincoln had been faintly talking, only slightly louder than a whisper. Peculiar, as if the optometrist didn't want the others in the open store to hear his revelation and remarks. It didn't make sense why he felt comfortable sharing with Kyros, but no one else.

Kyros selected his favorite frames and Lincoln headed into another room.

Lincoln returned with two identical pairs of glasses and handed them over. Kyros held them, inspecting the spectacles like a hair in the soup. Intrigued, Kyros asked, "How will the world look through these glasses?"

Jacob Yastrow

"Different enough to look at things differently that you never before thought twice about. It will quickly become evident that what you thought you saw in many lights appears wrong. Uncertainty and self-contradiction are inevitable and encouraged to grow fruitful. Clarity helps reveal truth. My truth is different today than yesterday, as yours will be when you walk out that door." Lincoln's eyes fixed on the exit sign.

The answer didn't suffice, and the way Lincoln spoke didn't seem to provide any insight. Throughout the experience Kyros' confusion had only grown. He wondered how he was supposed to make sense of the situation, let alone of the words spoken by the optometrist. Were the glasses supposed to help his eyesight or shift the fabric of his entire consciousness? Little did he know, things would begin to look differently in time.

The two walked over to a computer and Kyros handed over the money his mom had given him the night before.

When his palm started to push the door open, Kyros hesitated and wanted some guidance. He looked over his shoulder with both glasses still in hand. Neither pair had been tested. "What if I have trouble seeing with the glasses? What if I don't like what I see?" Kyros felt like he knew better than to ask another couple of questions that the answer might not seem to harbor the slightest assistance. However, he knew they needed to be asked.

Lincoln smiled, "With the right help you can fix both those problems. Try 'em out before you start your car. If you feel like you can wear them and still safely operate your vehicle, go for it."

As suspected, the answer provided no immediate aid. In the car he grabbed a pair and was pleased to be experiencing no dizziness or headache. The world was simply more detailed with mundane objects reflecting new captivating colors.

The engine revved and Kyros admired the spectrum of the flowers and birds that stood vibrant against the perfectly blue and white sky. The iridescent purple flash of a passing blackbird distracted him while turning right onto the highway. Both tires on the passenger side rammed onto the curb. There was a pop and the tires dropped back to the asphalt. The next turn off was an abandoned parking lot. His phone was dead, and he had no way to call his parents; the flat tire wasn't going to change itself.

Kyros began to fumble with the jack, which caught the attention of a haggard recluse who slowly approached. Astonishingly, the man spoke much more eloquently than the average bum and he seemed like such an unlikely candidate for the homeless lifestyle. Every word was spoken without much thought, but with more passion, meaning and confidence than anyone Kyros had ever encountered.

Was this man on a different intellectual level or had the boy just never taken the time to hear what the average person had to say? Most kids didn't speak more than nonsense and most adults criticized and ridiculed him to a level more than a teenager could bare. Not a day in his life had Kyros spoke to a homeless man as the words "homeless" and "bum" had always been presented as negative. It was unheard of for a person of status to compliment or pay any regards to individuals seen as such classifications, unless they were yelling something along the lines of "Get a job!"

Furthermore, the man was very pleasant to be around. A strong odor of weed, mildew and sweat was impossible to miss, but aside from the smell, Kyros found no negative qualities.

The man had an attention for detail and provided an impactful lesson. Kyros was shown how to check wear on the brake pads. Once the spare was on, Kyros learned how to inspect the oil and judge if he needed new oil or for the volume to be adjusted. There was also a brief lesson on suspension.

Kyros uncharacteristically expressed his appreciation for the help and merged back onto the highway. Homeless lifestyle was pondered, and he wondered if there were others like the helpful, intellectual and well-spoken man. He drove over Maya Bonita Creek as challenges of living on the streets played through his mind. They all appeared so miserable and pathetic, with their strong smells, dirt-stained skin, matted hair and tattered clothes.

Although it was a frequently traveled route, the sign had never stood out. His glasses allowed Kyros to see the faded words for the first time. The car slowed and halted in a pull off at milepost two hundred-sixty-two.

The woods got thicker, and beauty grew as Kyros walked upstream along Maya Bonita Creek. However, as with the beauty and awe, more trash in higher densities apparent with every step. The hill flattened, opening into a valley where a powerful river meandered through a lush wetland near a lake. Following the river north, he spotted a collection of trash next to a deteriorating building and an area with stumps of inconceivable size. The trees that once stood there must have been huge.

Dazzling flowers allured him over to a spiny blackberry thicket cloaking the upland environment. All the other plants had been choked out. It looked like Kudzu. Kyros approached and ate from the thorny mass, but something was wrong other than the veracity of the plants. More trash caught his eye and was poisoning the river. The banks were dotted with rotting catfish and the water was dark green. Not a live fish could be spotted. Downstream, pieces of trash floated in the thousands. Plastic and Styrofoam fragments accumulated at the dam. Beer cans and cigarette butts scattered like shrapnel. Fifty-five-gallon drums, tires and appliances in the shallows. A dead beaver over four feet in length with massive front teeth lay mostly eaten, presumably by the half dozen Turkey Vultures on the ground. More circled above.

The sun started to set and Kyros left the gruesome scene to head home. The air conditioner kicked on full blast and his sweaty back stuck to the leather seat. Oil wells dotted vast swathes of farmland. When the sun went down, fires danced on top of wells as excess methane burned across the horizon. A normal sight in the oil driven county, but the wells appeared more menacingly than they did yesterday. There were even some on his family's property. He started to get a headache.

He remembered a family trip a few years back when visiting his sister in Louisiana. The family wanted to see the mouth of the Mississippi River, hoping to see new landform from the deposited sediment.

Jacob Yastrow

Since New Orleans, the river hadn't come into view once.
All they could see were grassy levees that corralled the
current. After the last small town, they drove down a
deserted road surrounded by water. At least two different
oil refineries were clearly visible in the mouth of the river.
The environment was a wasteland.

Back in New Orleans they learned that historic alterations
to the delta created conditions that prevented the
formation of new land. Sediment didn't get carried
downstream from the floodplains once the river couldn't
flood. Also, the river was lined with numerous
overpopulated cities as opposed to a pristine
conglomeration of wetland and upland environments.

The lush, forested mountainside up Maya Bonita Creek was
a far prettier site than the Mississippi River Delta, and he
wasn't even sure how long those trees would remain.

His family's house used to be a half hour drive to the city
but in the last two decades the city expanded closer and
most of the surrounding forest had been cut to make way
for farms. His family had lived in the area since long before

the agriculture takeover. Faint memories of a child walking with his family through the woods for hours without seeing roads or other people flickered in his head. He looked through the trees at the seemingly endless expanse of farmland. He missed those woods and now it was only a short walk to the start of the massive farms.

A clearing broke, revealing a sizable chunk of nothing in the middle of the forest. The property was once home to the biggest tree in the area, but it was cut down a few years after rumor broke out – the land replaced by a soybean farm owned by Sam Jones.

The dashboard temperature gauge dropped six degrees as the Jones farm turned back to forest. From the bridge, he could see the remnants of the creek that flowed near his family's property. Until that year, Kyros had never even seen the riverbed. There had always been flowing water in his childhood.

In his room, Kyros felt compelled to write a poem about the oil wells that were all over the county.

Jacob Yastrow

Methane flares out of the wells

tapped deep underground

orange dances in the night across the plains

Flames flicker up from

streets of neighborhoods and towns

within a couple hundred yards of businesses and houses

Not the profile

commonly scene in these stories

they sit amongst white middle class communities

Most see no harms

of course fracking is the driving force of the economy

there's no way there can be risks

Babies grow up

in same boats as elderly and sick

more prone to suffer from exposure

A bliss exists

risen from ignorance

or illusion to self that there is nothing to fear

The wells that aren't in towns

sit near floodplains and on farms

that grow food for everything fed to the masses

The boy awoke to the smell of steak and realized he had fallen asleep for an hour. His fingers were numb, and his cheek and crooked glasses wet from drool. A glance in the mirror allowed Kyros to situate the glasses before opening the door.

"Oh, so now you've decided to join us." The tone of his mother almost sent him back upstairs. It was a little past eight.

A breath was taken. "Sorry Mom, I didn't sleep much last night. I also got a flat tire a few hours ago on my way back from the eye doctor."

His mother's mood shifted from frustrated to concerned. "Oh honey, are you alright?"

"Yes mom, a homeless man gave me a hand."

"A WHAT?" Raising her voice, his mother scolded, "Kyros, you need to be careful and can't be hanging around people like that."

"PEOPLE LIKE THAT?" The room was silent. His response even shocked him a little. He made eye contact with his mom and said, "The man was actually really nice and smart." His mom smirked and he continued, "My phone was dead and something in me trusted him. I felt like I could give him a chance."

"I certainly hope so. Are you sure he wasn't just trying to get money?"

"Mom, he didn't ask for anything."

The steak rested and his mom pulled the mashed potatoes from the oven. "Anyways, your father and I will let you borrow some money, and you can save up your allowance to pay us back."

"You're making me pay? Why can't you?"

"Honey, we give you a room, food, clothes, a car, gas money and a phone. You are seventeen and should be paying for all these things yourself. When I was your age, I had two jobs and helped my mom take care of my younger sisters. All you do is go to school, do a little homework, then sit around and have fun for the next six hours before you go to bed and repeat the process. You need some guidance and direction. You have too much time and it's doing you no good. You need to start thinking about getting a job so you can make some money. I don't like your attitude and you should be grateful you don't have to pay for more. There are things in this world given to you, but you must remember, money doesn't grow on trees and you can't get by without money."

Kyros plopped the biggest steak onto his plate and decided it wasn't worth it to argue. In a matter of minutes his plate was clean, and the ravenous boy violently cut into the extra steak in the middle of the table. An attempt to excuse himself early was stopped as his mom calmly spoke, "It's your turn for dishes."

The stagnant water in the sink brought him back to the polluted pond. He then thought about the reservoir that supplied the counties water. In the last few years, the shoreline receded more than any of the old-timers could remember.

It took several minutes for the water to get hot and for the first time, he connected household water consumption to the level in the lake. Everything was out of the sink and he started the dishwasher. Kyros wanted to know how much water it took to run one load. He had a conflicting internal debate to resolve if it was wasteful that so much water was used to clean off dishes only to put them in a dishwasher.

An internet search revealed the average water usage in an American household, and he was baffled. The use of water wasn't just water that flowed from the sink; it included water used for production of clothes, gasoline, food and numerous other uses. One site claimed that water for livestock, particularly cows, accounted for the largest proportion of water usage globally. The twenty ounces of steak he just consumed must have taken more water to produce than all the water his family used for dishes over the course of a week.

Kyros placed the glasses on the bedside table and drifted to sleep. He wasn't normally quick to adopt routines, but every day to follow, the glasses would be removed at night and set on his nose and ears the following morning.

Jacob Yastrow

Dreen Gesert

The next day at school Kyros was surprised that nobody ridiculed him about his glasses. While preoccupied with the eye doctor, the homeless man, the polluted pond, river and lake in the natural area and his water consumption, he drew a forested landscape and wrote a poem.

You came to my aid in a time of need
Your help allowed me to drive home
You weren't what I expected a homeless man should be
You spoke so fluid and eloquently
I believe you're different than what many think they see

Jacob Yastrow

An attempt to discretely tuck the note into his desk was made too late. Dreen Gesert reached in and pulled out a crinkled page. He started scanning. The paper was folded a few times and deposited into his pocket. "Come to my office after class."

A few students responded with "Ooooooohhh Kyros is in trouble."

Kyros walked into the north wing offices and asked an unfamiliar lady, "Do you know if Mr. Gesert is in his office?" He silently followed her towards his teacher's desk.

"Ah Kyros, I was just thinking about you." Mr. Gesert waved the poem. "What you have here is pretty interesting. I wrote a few notes but wanted to make sure to return this by the end of the day. I appreciate you coming to see me. You're an outstanding student with a world of potential. Your poem is beautiful. If you don't want to tell me that is fine, but who is this helpful man you wrote of?"

Kyros shrugged and after several seconds his teacher began again. "Anyways, I wrote a few notes that may help." Dreen seemed disinterested in hearing a response.

20

"What kind of notes?" Kyros didn't have a clue what to expect. He wondered if his teacher had made grammatical corrections.

"Some stuff that I think can help." Dreen's chair rolled back, and he grabbed his laptop. "I need to prepare for my next class. I'll see you on Wednesday." The teacher walked away leaving Kyros alone in the office. The vicinity was scanned and Kyros noted that the teacher looked obsessed with plants. There were pictures of him in front of numerous trees all across his desk.

Kyros flung his pack onto his right shoulder and strolled to the last class of the day. He tried making sense of the teacher's notes, but the meaning wouldn't be revealed for a few days.

Anticipation was building to understand the three notes on the drive home. In the solace of his bedroom, he looked up the first on his phone. Kyros typed "Bacchus Sophos," but it provided no incite. He then typed "Bacchus," and found out this was the Roman god of wine and intoxication

Jacob Yastrow

who was celebrated with a wild festival involving lots of sex and crime.

His search of "Sophos" revealed a definition, "wise or wisdom in regards to a certain skill or knowledge." On the page, below the note "Bacchus Sophos," Dreen had written a couplet. Kyros read it aloud. "Who decides who is the foolish or the wise, who determines the truth." Kyros was lost. Was his teacher referring to him as foolish or wise? Or was he in fact calling his student a liar? The first two notes tore at Kyros' mind until he could take no more. A break was needed, and the television served a relaxing escape.

The following day Kyros performed poorly on his history quiz. He studied and knew the answers, but Mr. Gesert's words clouded his mind. Temporarily distracted from the conundrum, the boy remembered that there was a third note. He pulled out the page with the poem and read, "6171994." Kyros slammed his hands on his desk and yelled "FUCK!"

The class became silent, and Mr. Bryce was livid. "Please step out to compose yourself and don't come back unless you are ready to engage in the discussion."

Kyros grabbed his belongings and stormed off toward Mr. Gesert's office. Kyros found out his teacher was gone for the day. He felt too distracted to attend class, so he drove home and asked his mom to call him in sick. He awaited getting to the bottom of his teacher's notes.

Class ended the following day, and Kyros knew he only had fifteen minutes before the next period. He rushed to the front of the room and pulled the poem out of his backpack. "What do you mean by these notes?"

"Well, what do you think I mean?" Dreen smiled.

Kyros despised having his questions answered with a question. He took a breath. "I looked up Bacchus Sophos and couldn't find anything. Then, I searched each word separately." He went on to explain the contradiction yielded from his search.

Jacob Yastrow

Dreen Gesert looked impressed. "You've almost got it. Now combine the second note with the contradiction you uncovered."

Shocked to see he made progress, Kyros reread the second note with increased confidence. "Who decides who is the foolish or the wise, who determines the truth." The significance of the two words in the first note grew apparent. He looked at his teacher and tried to put thought into words, but it took several seconds before he began. "Bacchus is the fool, even though he is god? And Sophos is wise." Kyros looked for reassurance and Dreen gestured to continue. "They argue with each other over who is right?"

"You're close, yet a little off. One who is wise wouldn't feel the need to argue or affirm whether he is right. I can also think of many men who were incredibly foolish, yet still idolized."

Kyros digested the words. He proceeded cautiously, "So... someone is judging the fool and the wise?"

"Bingo." Mr. Gesert looked pleased and helped some more. "Someone is judging, but look at how I spelled the first note with a capital 'B' and 'S.' So…"

Kyros could tell his teacher wanted him to finish the thought. "So… Bacchus Sophos is a name, and he is being judged by someone who thinks he is foolish and wise."

Mr. Gesert clapped and decided to provide exactly what he meant in his first two notes. "Society will try to impose a truth, while Bacchus Sophos knows his own truth. A truth society has is that Bacchus Sophos is a fool. However, Bacchus feels confident that he is, but a fool. The powerful name represents a struggle of identity and status. The class with monetary wealth thinks they are rich, while the man you speak of in your poem is poor. On the contrary, the man who helped you is rich with a different kind of wealth and sees the man with money as poor."

Kyros tried to wrap his head around his teachers' words. It was such a foreign concept, but the message seemed understandable.

Jacob Yastrow

Three bells chimed the end of the passing period. He wanted to know about the third note. As if his teacher could read minds, Mr. Gesert said, "Kyros, come to my office during lunch tomorrow. I need some help and I would also enjoy finishing my explanation of the notes if your grasp is still struggling."

"Wait. Really quick… how do I decide who is telling the truth? Also, how can I help you? You're the teacher and I'm only the student."

Dreen showed nearly every tooth and chuckled. "I can see you are still slightly foolish, but it's fine since you are still young. Only you can decide who tells the truth and who is the foolish or the wise.

"Don't let labels dictate reality. We can only learn through our own interpretations or from the interpretations and assistance of others. Any human can learn something from anyone, thing or experience. I'm sure you could "teach" at least a thing or two to any "teacher" in this school." Dreen again said "teacher" with two fingers, implying quotations.

"If anyone says otherwise, it's because their pride or arrogance blinds them from a truth.

"I can easily admit that my son helped me learn how beautiful life was when he was born. Later he helped me learn of primal human instincts as he crawled around on the floor, grasping objects, sticking them in his mouth. As he grew older, he helped me learn about new paradigms of his generation and societal advancements that I was too old to have learned from any of my "teachers" in school.

"There's no way you can't help me at all. Come talk to me tomorrow so we can help each other. I just need a hand carrying some things to my car, but no pressure." The teacher handed him a singed note that explained Kyros was late, because Mr. Gesert was helping him finish an assignment. Kyros gathered his belongings and headed to class.

The following period Kyros was too preoccupied to pay much attention. One of the smaller boys was sitting next to him with dirt on his knees and his hands were filled with minor cuts. Kyros blurted, "You're covered in dirt."

Jacob Yastrow

The small boy responded, "SHHH! You've been talking all class and I'm trying to listen. Some of us care about our grades."

A smirk preceded a brief giggle. Kyros excelled amongst his peers, scoring better and finishing before the boy and the bulk of his class on all tests and in-class activities. Eye lids lowered in a condescending manor and Kyros over spoke his teacher again to say, "I just want to know why you're dirty."

"If you gave a shit any day before this you would see that I am dirty and tired just about every day. I don't get to wake up and watch cartoons before school. Every morning I wake up, check on my crops and animals, and then do whatever needs to be done on my family's farm before I get to go to school."

Kyros was taken back by the words. *"Get to go to school..."* It didn't make sense. The last thing Kyros viewed school as was a privilege.

Right then, Kyros tuned back to the instructor's voice and realized ironically enough that the history of various

28

farming techniques was the topic of the day. Coincidence or Kyros had a hunch why the boy was dirty before he asked. The teacher explained the pros and cons of various land conversion methods for farming. A hand from the young boy next to Kyros shot like a rocket into the air. Pausing the lecture, Mr. Bryce warmly said, "Yes, Joel."

Joel responded by saying, "Really how effective are these methods? Sure, it may work, but for how long? One year, two years, three years, before the topsoil is lost and damaged from plowing, no more plant available nutrients exist in the baron soil and nothing can grow. The farmers will then abandon this plot of land and move onto the next. It isn't sustainable and is in fact very flawed."

Kyros' mind was blown. Based on the blank, baffled stare of his teacher and classmates, he wasn't sure how Joel knew what he said or if it was true.

Mr. Bryce took a breath and said, "It may not be the most environmentally friendly, but there is a lot of land in this world and this practice is optimal for many of the world's people."

Joel jumped back in. "How can you say that? Like I just stated: maybe optimal for the first year or two. My dad taught me about complexities of nature and how progress stops when an area of forest is clear-cut and/or slashed and burned to make way for agriculture. The soil, the root systems of trees, the plants themselves and the animals inhabiting the area can easily become lost."

The teacher was losing composure and didn't know how to recover. He raised his voice and said, "There isn't substantial evidence to support what you are saying. In reality, animals and plants don't lose significant portions of their range to farming and in many cases the land can and will be used to farm for decades, maybe more. I know of farms in the corn belt that have been growing food since the nineteen eighties." Kyros noticed that Joel looked disappointed as the topic changed.

When Joel turned and saw Kyros looking empathetic, Joel whispered, "This asshole doesn't know what he's talking about. You wanna see farming? Come home with me after school. I'll show you around and I'm sure my dad would be thrilled that one of my classmates is taking an interest in

30

the health of the planet and my family's livelihood. He'd be more than happy to explain whatever it is you want to know."

Kyros, for the first time in months. felt very fortunate and gladly remarked, "That would be cool," and gave Joel his phone number.

After school, Joel and his father came by Kyros' home and the boy eagerly slid into the backseat.

Jacob Yastrow

The Food Forest

From the backseat window, the approach was nothing short of spectacular. Four miles away, Joel's father, Palo, pointed off in the distance. "That square of lush land that you see on the other side of the river is our home." Palo, an ambitious man with great vision, knew the awe and splendor of his creation. Kyros would learn that Palo bought one hundred and thirty acres of neglected farmland next to the river thirty-five years earlier. At the time, there weren't more than a few dozen established trees and not much green other than the wet areas near the creek and river on the lower portions of the property. The forested patch was an oasis within the farmland. The entire county looked neglected, yet this family's home must've contained more shades of color than the

Jacob Yastrow

Appalachian's Blue Ridge Parkway. The tallest trees were approaching seventy-five feet.

The temperature dropped. Palo made sure to travel slowly with all windows down once they turned off county roads. So many sounds filled the air. A handful of different bird calls in the first minute. Each species of tree had its own sound, whether influenced by variances in the way leaves rustled in the wind, different animal inhabitants, fruit falling to the forest floor or from some other unique phenomenon that a human mind couldn't identify or perceive.

A family of deer ate various grasses by a small creek. Kyros could tell that it was once an irrigation ditch that had been repurposed. This waterway was man-made but barely discernible from one in a pristine forest. Ducks fled downstream at first glance towards the river.

The road veered away from the creek and ran parallel to the edge of a clearing, which an ecologist would've easily mistaken as a natural forest meadow, and not a three-acre blip of farmland in the middle of a planted forest.

Palo and Joel could tell that their guest was getting eager and smiles on their faces grew. Palo said, "For now, just take it in. All of your questions will be answered on the tour." Palo paused, "Too many people in this world limit their capacity and ability to take in the beauty of the world, because they are talking and trying to understand. Not enough people take in the beauty first. Enjoy the beauty and abundance and we'll start our tour at the house. If you'd like to check with your parents, you can even stay the night in our guest room tonight and see the rest of the property tomorrow."

The clearing was no longer visible, and a large pond came into view with a house on the far shore. Herons and egrets waded in the shallows. Geese lined the sunny Northeastern shore on a grassy area.

The landscaping around the home was immaculate with every color of foliage and flower. Not an inch had gone to waste, yet everything had enough space and didn't look cluttered. His hosts went inside while Kyros took it all in. After a few minutes Joel and Palo returned just as Kyros found the first bare patch of dirt since stepping out of the car.

"Kyros, Joel will show you the animals when he does evening chores, but for now he has a few things he needs to take care of. I'll give you a tour with an emphasis on the plants. Here are a couple apples and a jar of water in case you're hungry or thirsty. Dinner will be ready in a few hours. Do you have anything you'd like to ask before we begin?"

Kyros said, "Thanks! I'm really excited to learn about what you have going on and this is all so impressive. Your property is amazing, and I don't ever want to leave." The food was happily gobbled down, and the water jar stuffed into his back pocket.

Palo started to get teary and thanked the boy, welcoming him to return whenever he wished, as long as he offered a helping hand. "You can share all of the bounty of our space. There is more food than any of us could ever dream of."

"That's what I've been meaning to ask…" Kyros hesitated and wanted to choose the right words. "Where is…I mean where do you grow all of the food that supports your family? It looked like you only had a small area being used in the meadow we drove past. Do you have another part of the property that you farm?"

"You're looking at it, and in fact, we're standing in one of our most productive areas." Palo stretched his hand towards the descending sun and moved his arm gently over to the east where the full moon would soon rise. "Nothing we do is very conventional. Nothing we do replicates what you see outside of this haven in the surrounding landscape.

If you look closely you can see that our entire house is situated in the middle of a circle, broken into the four cardinal directions, north, east, south and west." Again, his arm slowly fanned across the landscape, but this time his body spinning in a full circle. "This is our Medicine Wheel Garden and our house is the totem in the middle. The center of the house has a fireplace with sacred stones from around the world. It is where we make our offerings."

"Are you Native American?" Kyros knew his question was a little silly by the shift in Palo's posture.

Palo placed his right hand over his left breast and took a breath. "Kyros, I want you to understand something. We are all native to this earth. Some come from different places and take what belongs to others, but all of our origins are similar. All humans once had a deep connection to the land. They were intimate and influenced by her patterns. Every section of year filled with actions, rituals and traditions that were associated and incorporated to utilize seasonal abundances and prepare for more difficult times like drought, famine, harsh winters, floods and times when animals would move. Humans followed the animals and became more and more sedentary as humans started to follow the greater patterns of the universe. Agriculture became more accessible as knowledge of the sun and seasons were utilized.

"Every human being alive on earth still has a primal self that is held on by the strings of our ancestry. We are connected to a primitive being that can never go away. At times, a relation unrecognizable, but always there. Both you and I likely didn't have a family member that was a farmer by occupation for maybe three to five generations, but that didn't stop me. Do you think my dad, grandfather or great grandfather was a farmer? They couldn't even grow a cactus if they tried." Palo laughed and gestured for Kyros to follow across the Medicine Wheel Garden.

Taken back by a personality so dissimilar than any ordinary person, Palo's motives and methods were confusing. Kyros was clueless why this man was, as Lincoln, so open and sincere. The homeless man, too, maintained honest and authentic expressions in a way that was a stark juxtaposition to what seemed like every other interaction that Kyros had ever had with an adult. Was this how people were supposed to communicate and that within his small circle nobody spoke as such?

A few steps later, the humble man glanced at Kyros and kept explaining, "You don't need to be Native American to make offerings. You don't need to be Native American to see value and beauty in their culture and spirituality. You don't even need to be Native American or native anything to respectfully adopt aspects from that region, whether it is Sumerian culture, Chinese, the Vedas, Celtic, Mayan, aboriginal Australian or elsewhere. Even if you aren't a direct descendent of that culture, the culture is respected and preserved. I can't think of a truly spiritual man of any culture that would have an issue with me constructing a Medicine Wheel Garden, growing the three sisters, making offerings to our totem or having my church, priest, rabbi and meditation all be my garden and the land.

"It doesn't matter who you are, where you come from, what you have done, what others have imposed on you or aspirations that any individuals or institutions have of you. What matters is that you follow your heart, but don't neglect the mind. The mind is the greatest servant, as long as it isn't the master. But the heart… let your heart guide. If you want to grow food, grow food. If you want to respectfully adopt aspects of other cultures and traditions, past and present, then do it. If you want to go to college and become a doctor, physicist or lawyer, then go do that. Let it be your choice. Let your heart speak.

"If I adopted the lifestyle that my family and society wanted, I wouldn't be here. I wouldn't have land. I wouldn't know how to grow food. This hundred-thirty-acre plot that I bought thirty-five years ago would look just like every other parcel in this county if I hadn't defied the aspirations of others. I have arborists, ecologists, agriculture experts, city planners and many others who travel from all over the world to see this food forest."

"Food forest?" Kyros was with Palo every step of the way until he heard this foreign concept.

Palo's cheerful demeanor and smile returned. "That's what this is. That's the answer to your question about how there is enough food grown here to support ourselves. You are standing in the most complex and developed edible food forest in the country. I can tell you that just about every plant growing on the entire property is either edible, medicinal or both.

"Traditionally in nature, just about every plant has either edible or medicinal properties to varying degrees. Even in the Sonoran Desert in Arizona, there are relatively very few plants that should never be consumed for any reason.

"Unfortunately, most commercially used landscaping plants in this country are so modified and cross bread to select advantageous traits that they have slowly lost their nutritional and medicinal properties. Cities all over have thousands of fruit trees, or more, that are strictly ornamental and don't even produce fruit. Not to mention, that are dosed with toxic fertilizers, fungicides and pesticides.

"The plants you see here are the real deal. Many of my fruit trees and woody plants are very old varieties that have been preserved for decades, sometimes generations, simply by grafting. You would be amazed at all of the plants you can propagate for free with one simple cut from the mother plant. Sure, you need to know how to propagate and graft, and make sure you have optimal varieties and rootstocks for your specific spot, but with the right knowledge, many foods, medicinal and landscaping plants become as inexpensive as the supplies to propagate.

"Herbs, shorter lived plants and plants that are hard to propagate, but possible to germinate, I grow from seeds. I have plant varieties from all over the world and have planted seeds from the plants in their naturalized or native domain. For instance, if I can't get seeds from India, I get seeds that are grown by reputable growers that have environmentally and socially ethical practices. I make sure that they are not genetically modified but are organically grown without harmful chemicals, if they aren't sustainably wildcrafted. Some of my heirloom varieties I've grown for decades and haven't seen another of that variety from any other farmer or grower in at least that long.

"Every year dozens of varieties of plants are lost – forgotten in the name of simplicity. Massive agriculture conglomerates are profit driven. They spend so much on their mechanized farming inputs and labor that per acre, they can't afford to make anything short of the most profitable. Each additional variety of corn or lettuce means that much variation in the needs of the plant. To make things easy, they genetically modify and crossbreed to get a crop that can grow prolifically, productively, handle toxic chemicals and flourish in just about any condition. Seven of my twelve squash varieties have never been grown commercially in this country, other than for small scale seed production and distribution.

"This food forest we are in would be self-sustaining if we were to no longer intervene, but we joyously take part and nurture the organism as a whole and all of the parts respectively. We help build soil; certain plants we prune or cut-back for better food production; we continually tend to our annual food and medicinal crops to make sure they prosper; we collect their seeds in some varieties and leave many more to do the reseeding themselves.

"Plants don't just grow on the horizontal plane, but also grow vertically like a lush rainforest. We have the upper canopy at about seventy feet. Below that, over twenty species and eighty varieties of fruit, nut and medicinal trees make up the next layer. Dwarf fruit trees and large shrubs grow in the space between and below, with small shrubs and annual and perennial plants on the ground. There are even more layers. There is the rhizosphere, which is made up of plants that grow harvestable parts below ground. These include, but aren't limited to, ginger, ginseng, carrots, radishes and potatoes.

"Additionally, there are vines and the ground cover. All of the layers work together, allowing minimal input once the organism is supported for a certain amount of time. Ground cover and low light penetration prohibit weeds from growing.

"Soil that is covered and not exposed increases moisture and water retention, as does each additional inch of organic matter. We don't till. When we harvest or remove a plant, we often add compost and plant a successive plant immediately. I can tell you that the average farm in the Midwest has less than a couple inches of organic matter, yet I've measured over two feet deep in many of my most productive beds. Also, I want to note, we try not to use pesticides. The last time we applied one, was an organically grown habanero pepper, that we cut up, boiled in water and strained into a spray bottle. In at least the last year, that is the only pesticide that I have applied.

"Remember, plants work together. There is a concept called companion planting in which you plant certain plants together or away from another to promote well-being and reduce pest populations. Nitrogen fixers, which include all legumes, provide nitrogen. Compost and accumulated organic matter provide the bulk of the other essential and trace nutrients. I haven't fertilized with anything other than compost from my animals and green manure from my cover crops for over ten years now.

"On the way up the driveway you might've noticed a familiar plant, corn, growing with a couple other plants."

Kyros nodded and Palo resumed full speed, but not overwhelmingly fast. "Traditionally corn would be grown alongside squash and pole beans. The corn would provide the shade for the squash and the scaffolding for the beans.

The beans would fix nitrogen and the squash a protective barrier and ground cover to reduce predation and desiccation.

"Certain plants deter or attract pests, and many can be used to form barriers. In the meadow, I'm sure you saw the rows of plants that were growing between the different sections of field and pasture. The plants there provide some different functions. They slow the flow of water in the event of heavy rain and filter out runoff nutrients from our animals before entering the creek and river.

"I don't need fences between plots, because the dense shrubbery prohibits the alpaca, horses and goats from roaming between patches. I have small areas cut with gates for when I need to move the animals around."

They stood in the Medicine Wheel Garden for a quiet minute. Kyros was digesting all the information and Palo didn't need a response. Palo was truly gifted in sharing and showing knowledge. "Palo, thank you for sharing with me. I had no clue about all of this. I want to learn and see more, but I don't want to take up too much of your time."

Jacob Yastrow

Tears began to develop again on the middle-aged man's face. "I have all the time in the world to share my heart and mind with you."

All the information was a revelation and the content so different than ordinary dialogue. Kyros had to ask, "I am very grateful and appreciative for your patience and compassion, but there is something that I need to know. Why are you sharing this with me? Is this the same tour and information you share with all of your guests?"

Palo silently contemplated his response. "Most people are too blindly governed by that which is assigned to them to have the capacity to share genuine connection with something or someone significantly removed from their network of reality. Most people, I could introduce my words, time and heart, and they either wouldn't value it or they would lack understanding, ignore, dismiss or some combination. Most people aren't fond of learning their understandings and lifestyles could be contradictory than what they have been indoctrinated into believing.

"I have tried to present my understandings and personal lessons to the many, but the many don't believe me and they don't believe in me. I sense our stories share common ground. Most of your greatest gifts I feel have been diminished and unvalued, just like me, whenever we have attempted actual communication and connection within conventional society.

"Only those truly unconventional in action, mind or heart in at least one way can possess the capacity to receive what I can give. I can tell you are truly interested in understanding and not judging and that is why I'm open to sharing my time with you. It's okay if people have disagreements, what's important is that we can communicate and bridge understandings."

Kyros didn't disagree, but speculated if Palo really understood him. Kyros didn't even know himself well enough to understand all the ways he was like this unconventional caretaker of the food forest. He felt strongly that he never really had been valued and it hurt. Kyros, unusually and for the first time, felt like he was actually doing the right thing, despite what he had been convinced in his youth and teens.

 The boy remembered that Palo went on a tangent and didn't even explain the garden they were standing in. "I never really thought about these ideas, but I think you're right and I am starting to see some of the ways that we stand in similar shoes. We really aren't as different as I thought despite our age and demographics. I have to express how impacting this is for me. I'm not just a kid to you and no adult has made me feel that."

Palo smiled and Kyros continued, "I'd love to continue the tour, but first, can you explain to me what a Medicine Wheel Garden is?"

"It's a garden divided into four sections based on the cardinal directions, with a totem or monument of value placed in the center. For us, it is our house with our fireplace. Each section is broken into plants of different colors.

"When constructing, the designer, like most things, can follow traditions and replicate a certain regions Medicine

Wheel Garden, or you can create it in a way most harmonious and compatible with your heart. There are a few things I recommend keeping consistent. You want to have an outer circle, resembling a closed wheel that is generally divided into four sections. Pick a spot that is sacred and special. Don't force a spot; let the spot present itself. Have a monument or altar in the middle for offerings – a spot where people can leave a stone or gift when they visit the wheel. Other than that, the world is yours. The wheel is to be a place of peace. If conflict or issues arise within, calmly leave the circle and resolve affairs outside of the healing space." Palo paused and asked, "Is that a sufficient explanation?"

"Absolutely! That is really interesting. I want to spend some time looking at some different examples."

Palo nodded and walked over to the far end of the garden. Kyros followed him up a staircase that snaked between some cherry trees and into a chestnut. Ten feet up on the platform and Kyros could see a few remaining cherries dangling in all five trees -- withered away like the surrounding landscape outside of the blissful oasis. On what Palo referred to as the picking deck, two hardy kiwi vines climbed up the support posts on opposite ends around thirty feet apart and draped over circular tables with benches.

The trunk rose up through the middle of the upper platform forty feet skyward. When they made it to the top of the stairs the ground was over twenty feet below. Grapes climbed up the trunk and along the railings. The chestnut the masterpiece in the center. In each corner of the deck sat a potted plant pointing in a cardinal direction. Ripe grapes hung in front of the lush landscape.

To the west, the sun slowly descended. A faint outlined town, with taller buildings in the further distance, stood seemingly lifeless against the radiant sun. Back against the tree, Kyros watched Palo's presumably routine salutation for the evening. "Thank you, sun, for another day. Thank you for blessing this land with abundance, good fortune and our new friend, Kyros." Turning shoulders revealed the face of a modest man who waved the student over to the railing to face the radiant and blinding ball of fire.

Kyros walked over and Palo spoke some more. "Like the sun, as all things, a duality exists in humanity. Yin and yang compliment and complete fully. The world you know is different than the world on this land." Palo paused with outstretched hands for dramatic effect. "Different than the path which you are now heading." This time he powerfully brought his hands together, clasping for a second, before pointing his right index finger to the center of Kyros' chest. "Your journey is just beginning. Follow me."

The two of them meandered back down to the forest floor. For the first time, Kyros' was perceiving his entire being vibrating harmoniously with his surroundings. He didn't know it at the time, but not once in his seventeen years, other than with his mother, had he shared such a bond with a human, situation or experience. Even the connection with his mother hadn't come close in at least a decade. Kyros wondered if the man could see his future.

The feeling, Kyros could only compare to butterflies in his stomach. However, the tingly feeling occupied every cell of his being. Resonating at the exact same pitch, tone and frequency, with the same true and honest intentions, Kyros fit amidst the universe like one of the countless stars. He simply was in the same perfection as voices in a gospel choir. His heart and soul were singing, and he was glowing.

The walk across the forest was silent and lasted several minutes. Palo closed an eye and placed his hand between his face and the horizon. "Little over an hour till it gets dark. I'll show you the wetland and then Joel will show you the animals and evening chores before dinner." Palo stopped at the edge of the forest. "This is the largest wetland for at least two hours in every direction."

The statement didn't have the faintest impact on Kyros. Wetland was a word Kyros recognized but didn't fully understand. The astounding variation of the land was baffling and the shimmer of the sun glistening off the water surreal. Kyros gazed at the beauty. After a minute he asked, "What's a wetland?"

"A wetland is an area that is influenced by water yet inundated by less than a certain quantity of water for certain periods of time. They range in size, structure and productivity. For the sake of time, I'll let you borrow a great work of literature to better your understanding.

"Historically, wetlands have been among the least desirable ecosystems in the not so United States. Different interests sought to destroy and fill in any and all wetlands that weren't developed or converted into farms. The "Man" convinced the public, by framing wetlands as malaria breeding grounds, and campaigned to drain them all.

"A duality of wetlands exists, as well, as among all things. A great tragedy is an eye that only acknowledges and acts on part of the whole. Wetlands most often have standing or stagnant water that is used as breeding grounds for mosquitos that transmit malaria, West Nile and other infectious diseases. They stand collectively as close to if not the most productive landscapes. Wetlands contain more animal and plant diversity than either lakes or land individually.

"Transition zones are so important in nature. In any ecosystem you can find transition zones that have similar and unique microclimates, characteristics and species from the surroundings. If you look out across this lower area in the landscape, you can see more diversity than most places you've ever been. A lake, several ponds, a few channels, grassy hilltops with thriving prairie dog populations, willow and cottonwood groves, the large oak tree in the middle and shrubby hillsides that transition into cattails and other semi-aquatic plants. Thirty some acres – over a quarter of all my land – I restored and expanded wetlands that would've existed over a hundred years ago. I used wetlands from all over the Midwest to model the land in front of you."

Kyros reflected again on the trip to the mouth of the Mississippi River. What should've been abundant, lush wetlands, instead were levees, open water and oil refineries. The Mississippi was the largest watershed in the United States and the wetlands around the delta should have been vastly more complex than even Palo's.

The tangent in Kyros' thought came to a close as Palo began speaking again. "Nature thrives in peace and harmony with us on our land. Because there is so much prime native habitat and a diversity of differing habitats, the prey and predator populations stay in check. The deer stay moving and the small mammals don't go out into the open. I have next to no issues with animals destroying the plants I grow, for they are grown for them as much as me. I don't own this land and it is no more mine than any of theirs. By making sure the plants have what they need, the animals have all they need. I have plants throughout the land that I leave completely for the animals. I strategically plant in areas with good visibility, moderate cover, and easy access directly along the paths the animals frequently travel. I studied the unique tracks, scat and indications of seventeen medium to large mammals, cataloged sightings of fifty-two species of birds and a few reptiles and amphibians in my first two years on the land before such plantings."

On the edge of the expanse of wetlands, two men spoke as equals, resonating in harmony. Although Kyros was obviously younger and less experienced, his gifts were equally as impressive and vast. He was no more or less than Palo. Kyros was yet to understand this, or even begin to make sense of all the feelings and energy, but Palo saw

Kyros' potential, and that was the first time anyone had ever recognized that potential.

When Kyros' mom sped up the driveway, peace began to fade. Life was slow and pleasant since his arrival to the food forest three hours earlier. Joel's family was sad to see their new, to be, lifelong friend departed before dinner and animal duties, but understood that his mother already expected Kyros at another gathering. Palo said, "No need to apologize. You and I only get one mother in this life."

Kyros slid in the back seat, eager to tell his mom about the experience. Immediately, he felt discontent. His Mom and Grandma were far from the same page as him - in fact, not even in the same book.

At dinner, with more family members, seemingly all on a collective wavelength different than his, Kyros retracted his nourished heart and felt no desire to share. He ate silently, chiming in occasionally to respond to a question or request to pass the butter.

Understanding Bacchus Sophos

Mr. Gesert was talking to another student during the only free time Kyros had the following Monday. Kyros headed to lunch but was determined to gain a greater context to the perplexing notes despite Mr. Gesert's schedule.

Kyros turned off the highway on his way home from school to learn more about the homeless man who helped him. The young man fearlessly crossed through an encampment numbering over a hundred heads. Distraught and delusional individuals pulled at his arms and shirt, asking for money. He gave his only few dollars to an elderly woman too soon to realize he made a mistake. More homeless men and women started closing in.

Luckily, a man in his thirties approached and stood beside Kyros, telling them that the boy was a friend with nothing else to give. They reluctantly dispersed and the man took Kyros over to another group of people closer to the river and introduced himself. "Hello, young sir. I recognize you from the other day when you got a flat tire. My name is Planao, or wanderer in Greek." Pointing to the three people sitting around a trashcan fire he continued his introduction. "These great minds are Zeus, who is our so-called leader, Demeter – she grows our food, and this is Apollo – our healer."

Kyros was skeptical. "So, you're telling me that the three of them are gods and goddesses?"

None of them appeared like they minded his condescending remark. Planao gestured for Kyros to sit with them. Not wanting to offend, Kyros complied. "Planao, Zeus, Demeter and Apollo are our respective Greek names that we have picked for ourselves and each other. We have traditional American names but choose not to use them. What is your name, sir?"

Kyros didn't get why Planao kept calling him "sir."

"Ahh Kyros…the name many great men have had before you. Many not-so-great men too…"

The way Planao spoke was strange. Kyros understood that they chose Greek names, but why the names of gods and goddesses.

Planao continued, "The man who helped you change your tire goes by Bacchus Sophos."

Kyros was stunned. Mr. Gesert had known exactly who the poem was about and that's why he extended a hand. Dreen had done it to aid in Kyros' realization. Kyros asked, "Do you know Dreen Gesert?"

Zeus spoke, "Yes, but we know him as Green Desert. He goes by Dreen Gesert, which is only a pseudonym."

Kyros started to get it and responded, "Green Desert is a contradiction like Bacchus Sophos. Bacchus Sophos is the drunk or fool and the wise, while Green Desert is the forest and the desert."

"Life and death." Demeter raised her right hand. "I gave him that name. As an educator, I knew it was him who could provide salvation in the education system wasteland that you have come to know all too well. Green wanted to reach youth who struggled with identity and you stood out to him. When you showed up to class wearing glasses, Green picked up that you were ready to be reached."

"But Demeter," Kyros interjected. "It wasn't my glasses, but my poem about Bacchus Sophos that caught his attention."

"Yes, Kyros, but aren't those two of the same thing? Your glasses give you a different perspective of the world you have been seeing, while your encounter with Bacchus Sophos gave you a new perception of homeless people.

"There are homeless individuals like the ones over there..." pointing to a group nearby "...that are what you generally think of when you think of homelessness, but there are also homeless individuals like us." She looked at the others in the circle.

"Well then, why are you guys homeless? You all seem smart and capable. Bacchus Sophos came off to me as one of the most intelligent, clever and witty people that I've ever met. You all don't seem like you can be too far behind him if you're his good friends."

"Kyros," Demeter's soft voice came off her lips like a soothing river current. "You may see us and hold the heart to hear our souls despite societal illusions. However, those illusioned by society often have the hardest time understanding, recognizing and receiving our greatest gifts that us, Bacchus and Green have persistently persevered to spotlight. We all spent the first thirty years of our lives in the rat race and individually came to a convergent consensus that binds us in unity. Our families, bosses and superiors lacked the heart to appreciate or tune in to our blessings. Green was the only one who could keep his job in a way that could value him and allow him to achieve the highest. With many in this country, we are a canary in a coal mine when alone. But together, mirrors focus light to magnify our gifts naturally without societal abstractions and obstructions."

Zeus spoke before Kyros finished digesting, "You may have noticed all of our names are Greek except for the name Bacchus. Bacchus himself chose the name for his own reasons. In school he would get so drunk, and he was also Jewish, so his close friends called him Jewbacchus. Bacchus was the Roman god of Wine and Fertility. With aging, the name Bacchus alone, as he wanted it to mean, became a representation of the contradiction of the fool he was in High School and the god whom he was named after.

"Bacchus saw contradiction in man the fool and god the wise. Bacchus, the god of wine, influences people to become fools through intoxication, yet it was the foolish humans who were the first to perceive the wise and revered deities and also possess the capacity to interpret and share.

"As if Bacchus hadn't created enough of a conundrum for himself and us, he added the name Sophos – meaning wise or wisdom. He saw all aspects of Bacchus as foolish, so he finally concluded that he wanted to go by Bacchus Sophos."

Kyros looked as though his brain stopped working.

Zeus responded compassionately. His deep voice, pure. "I know it's confusing, but all the details don't matter. What is important is that you know who decides the foolish or the wise and who determines the truth."

The couplet from Kyros' teacher had been presented again.

Kyros asked, "Where did you get that?"

Demeter Smiled. "From Green. He came up with it after he met Bacchus Sophos on June 17th, 1994."

The numbers were a date. It all made sense. The first note was a name; the second was an interpretation of the name and *6171994* was June 17th, 1994. The past few days came full circle and Kyros finally felt at ease.

He left the group with confidence, ready to show his teacher what he had learned.

Jacob Yastrow

Kyros entered the office the following day at lunch. "Hello, Green Desert."

"Kyros, I'm impressed. I see you spoke with Bacchus Sophos."

"Not since Sunday, but I did meet your friends, Planao, Zeus, Demeter and Apollo. I also know what happened on June 17th, 1994."

"Bravo, Bravo. The fool is learning. Soon you'll determine what truth is, but first you must find your truth. I'm late for lunch, but I'll talk to you later."

Kyros was left in the office again and found it odd that his teacher said, "I'll talk to you later." Green Desert was starting to seem more like a friend than a teacher. The twenty-six pictures were glanced at once more, but this time the trees were all briefly admired. After the food forest visit, Kyros recognized one of the pictures was a small chestnut tree.

That evening, Kyros sat in deep reflection for some time before he identified a few truths. He was seeing the world

66

differently than ever before. He knew that he was outraged about the degradation of the natural area along Maya Bonita Creek; he knew not all homeless people were like what society had taught him to perceive; he knew he would no longer want to consume as much meat and dairy; and he knew he would no longer let labels dictate reality. He also knew that he was mystified and intrigued by food forests and trees. His last realization of the evening was that he wanted to be a light for the world, like Green Desert. Kyros didn't know what being a light entailed, nor the slightest clue how he would do so.

During the night, Kyros had a couple peculiar dreams. In the first, he was walking through a snaking path lined with velvet ropes. Something kept him moving forward. A hallway bisected on his left. Kyros ducked under the guide and headed down the hall. The right wall was lined with pictures. One was of him with a crooked hat and a college diploma. The next was a picture of what looked like to be an older version of him in an office. He had a large smile and was holding a paycheck with four digits. Kyros walked past the first two pictures and came to a gold-framed picture of a large house with a lush green yard, a wife, dog and two children. It looked like the man in the picture was himself around forty, but it had an unsettling mood. Kyros noticed the man in his American Dream home had bags under his eyes and looked miserable. The dream presented a man that looked like he had it all, but was missing so much. The next picture was a man in a large office with a grand view. On the desk were pictures of his kids trying to walk, little league games, piano recitals, prom dates and wedding photos. Kyros sensed this wealthy man was himself living the American Dream, while in turn missing major milestones and events in the lives of his own children playing out on the desk. The last picture on the right was a rock sitting on the bottom of a river.

Shortly after the rock in the river, pictures began on the left side of the hallway. The same river was flowing with Bacchus Sophos and the four others he'd met the previous day sitting on the bank. The next was him working in a food forest, harvesting peaches, sweat dripping from his face. He looked exhausted, but with a smile bigger than any he'd ever displayed before. The last picture was him in front of an audience. Everyone in the crowd cheered. The picture spoke to him so deeply. He could feel that he had pure and honest intentions and was fully connecting with the many.

He awoke and used the bathroom. Asleep again, he dreamt he was in the natural area picking up the countless pieces of trash with Green Desert. Suddenly, the two were in Green's classroom discussing sustainable living with several other intelligent and well-spoken men that were all on their own spiritual journeys. Palo stood in the circle with a wide smile. Everyone shared their dreams and goals. Kyros kept saying his dream was to live as lightly on this earth as possible, with the ability to grow all his own food, make his own clothes and tools, giving up unnecessary things that he couldn't produce himself. His goal was to help heal societal and environmental injustices and to be a model for others to follow.

Jacob Yastrow

Returning to Abundance

The food forest was even more beautiful than Kyros remembered. Even in late March, a full palette of colors and smells filled the oasis. The buds and bare bark of every tree as well as the flowers and unfurling leaves of other species gave each one a unique and discernable identity. He hadn't been out to the property for months, but Joel offered an invitation that Kyros couldn't pass up.

Palo was welcoming Kyros before he was fully out of the vehicle. "Welcome, my friend. Can we get you anything?"

"Palo!" Kyros closed his driver door and gave the man a hug. "Thank you, maybe in a little bit, but first I am very excited to learn about planting seeds."

Joel's father grinned and replied, "What kind of seeds?"

Jacob Yastrow

Kyros was slightly confused. "I thought you invited me here to learn how to plant fruit and vegetable seeds in the greenhouse?"

"We did, but you are also learning about planting seeds for the future."

"What do you mean?"

Palo shifted his stance. "Sometimes the slightest actions, gestures and experiences lay the very basis of a foundation that is somewhere between good and not so good. By following your heart and intention, just like planting an heirloom tomato seed in soil, you cultivate the garden of your life, which will nourish you with abundance and opportunity. By helping us plant seeds today, you are planting your first seeds in hands on gardening experience, I imagine, ever. You are furthering your relationship with our family in our home and the land. Words you say to others become planted seeds. Follow up words or actions, such as you visiting here today, allow you to tend to and nourish your seedlings and make sure they have enough intention and attention that they become fruitful and abundant within themselves. All seeds need enough support, but not too much. A fine dance between neglect and smothering, as with just about most."

"Okay…That's interesting. I see what you're saying. I'll think about it while I'm planting this morning."

"Sowing seeds is indeed meditative. Let's head to the greenhouse. Grab your water bottle if you have one. It gets hot in there midday." Palo turned and started walking toward the glass building on the hill.

Kyros grabbed his water bottle and followed. He wasn't sure if Palo was talking about literal or metaphoric sowing of seeds being meditative.

Garrett was well on the way with the daily plantings. He had already prepared soil in enough trays for several hundred individual plants. "Welcome, Brother." Garrett had long and curly brown hair with short, maintained facial hair.

Kyros greeted the man and shook his hand. Palo let Garrett know that the new blood had absolutely no farming experience and he would need to be filled in. Garrett carried a strong presence and was a gifted helper.

Garrett had no qualms towards sharing with the new student and he gave two thumbs up as Palo left the greenhouse.

"Where is he going?" Kyros asked.

Garrett smiled, "Brother Palo is full of life and works hard sunrise to sunset. Never have I seen another man with such stamina and dedication. He's off to do something. Hard to say what something exactly." Only briefly pausing, "So let's get started. We got lots to do. We are going to plant five hundred cells of lettuce and then I'll show you how to prep the soil before we seed squash."

Kyros thought to himself how that seemed like more lettuce than he'd consumed in his entire life.

"First, we need to poke a hole in every cell. Next, we will place six to ten seeds in each cell, before gently covering the seeds without applying significant pressure to the surface of the soil. As we finish each tray of plants, we will put a Popsicle stick in it with the crop name, variety and planting date, all labeled with a marker. At the end of each variety, we will write the same information, along with the total number of cells in the notebook with redwood trees on the cover."

Garrett grabbed a tray of soil and explained as he demonstrated. "You can use a lot of different things to poke the holes, but I prefer to use the end of the sharpie. If the cells are an inch or bigger across, you can use your fingers." He placed eight fingers across the bottom row of the tray and sped through the tray in twenty seconds with eight at a time. "You don't need to worry about going as fast as me today. It is about the experience. If you help seed in the future you can work on your speed, but for now just take it all in and feel free to try different techniques.

"As for depth, a general rule of thumb is to plant roughly twice as deep as the diameter of the seed. Small seeds, like lettuce, do great about an eighth of an inch deep, but bigger seeds, like the squash we'll start later, prefer to be an inch deep. Most plants will do just fine at half to quarter of an inch deep, unless they are small like lettuce, carrots or mint, or big like beans or sunflower seeds. Not all plants are started in the greenhouse. Many plants don't transplant well and some just do better if we plant the seeds directly in the ground after the last frost.

"There are also much more haphazard techniques to sowing. There is a principal from Japanese man that involves mixing sometimes over a hundred species of plants and fungi into clay pellets that are scattered across the landscape. He believed all will grow where they grow best if you give everything an equal chance. This is a practice that Palo has recently started to learn about, but the book by the Japanese man is a much better resource."

Garrett grabbed a bag of seeds from the table and poured a little pile in both his and Kyros' right hand. While talking, Garrett had poked holes in two trays and there was one in front of each of them. "Just grab a little pinch of the seeds and sprinkle them straight into the hole. It's okay if you pour twenty seeds instead of ten on accident. The effort it takes to remove the excess seeds isn't worth it."

Garrett finished in a minute and gently brushed soil from the edge of each hole over the seeds. He took the tray over to some others and inserted a labeled Popsicle stick, then grabbed two more without holes poked yet and set them on the table. By this point, Kyros had finished with his first tray. Garrett showed the way he gently covered each seed with soil, sometimes sprinkling more soil into the cell if there wasn't enough, without ever applying more pressure than the weight of his flat fingers. Kyros could hear Garret gently whispering and singing to the future plants to be.

The tray was labeled, placed with the others and Kyros was given a tray to himself. Poking holes with the piano technique seemed a little invasive and intense at first, so all seventy-two holes were poked with a sharpie. Garrett completed the other five trays in the time it took Kyros to do one and it was perfectly okay.

Next, they grabbed ten trays with twenty-four cells for the squash. Garrett spoke for the first time in a couple of minutes. "Plants like the lettuce, we plant weekly from

February through the first of October. Others like squash, peppers, melons, and tomatoes we will do one or two plantings at the start of the season and they will provide abundance until at least the first frost." The cells for the squash were significantly bigger than the lettuce. A twenty-four-cell tray of squash was the same size as the seventy-two-cell lettuce tray. Garrett told him the pots for tomato seeds were four inches across and deep. On another table there were tomatoes that had been started in February that were already eight inches tall and the average last frost was still two weeks away. There were hundreds of tomatoes in the greenhouse and there was still snow on the ground outside.

The squash varieties were much easier to plant and Kyros cruised through two trays of Spaghetti Squash in about five minutes. Together they planted forty-eight cells of field pumpkins as well as four varieties of other squash, including Yellow Crooked Neck, zucchini and Honey Dessert Delicata.

Garrett showed Kyros the soil mix that was in several large bags at the end of the greenhouse. "Before we put the soil in the trays, we need to moisten it and make sure there are no sticks or trash. We get a pallet of starting soil every year delivered from the local nursery. To moisten, we simply poor half a bag into this wheelbarrow and lightly water, while mixing with a shovel or my hands.

"Once it is wet, but not dripping, we thoroughly fill the cells. I put a few handfuls over the tray and level off the excess like a cup of flour with a knife. Then, I gently tap the tray on the table to make sure the soil settles to the bottom of each cell. If more soil is needed before the holes are poked, add more so each cell is full. Many people formulate their own starting soil, but I find it much easier to buy it. I don't love buying it, but our friends own the local nursery and formulate the blends themselves."

After an hour and a half in the greenhouse the plants were seeded and documented in the notebook. Garrett grabbed the watering wand that was attached to a long green hose. "No matter what seeds you sow, or if they're metaphoric, it is very important to water them in when finished. For the seeds to germinate, the soil needs to stay moist, without flooding. Once the seeds sprout in a week to two, water as needed, allowing the soil to dry out between thorough watering. We try not to water anything once the sun's angles get low to reduce chances for mildew and other fungal issues. Between ten and two is the time frame when most plants are most likely going to need water. Outside of that time frame the plants seem to do just fine. If nothing in the greenhouse is wilting at four p.m. in the middle of summer, then it is very unlikely that it will wilt between then and ten the following morning.

"It is also very important to consider water drop size. It isn't something that is regularly thought about or discussed even amongst the agriculture community, but it is very important. Most obviously, drops that are too big will wash out your cells and erode the soil, especially on the first watering. Additionally, water droplet size influences the way that water infiltrates and percolates through the soil. Big drops often run over the surface and don't even enter into the soil. When they do, the water will channel through select spots of the cell or soil profile without saturating entirely, but instead only fractions of it. I have watered cells that were very dry and the water flowed right out. When I came back twenty minutes later, plants had wilted more than before I watered. Using small droplets prevents erosion and allows the water to slowly enter and distribute throughout the soil. When the soil is especially dry, often I will go over and water the cells three or four times to make sure they get adequately and fully saturated."

Water began to flow out of the wand and Garrett gently moved it back and forth over the newly planted seeds several times without keeping the water in one spot for more than half a second. The wand fluidly cast an even dispersal of water across all the cells. The squash cells took more time and water to saturate than the lettuce. After watering the new squash and lettuce trays, Kyros was impressed to watch Garrett, able to selectively water all the tomatoes starts in a few minutes. He seemed to just look at the plants on the table and know the fifteen or so percent that he was going to water amongst the hundreds.

Kyros asked "How did you know which tomatoes to water?"

Garrett grinned and said, "They told me. The sad ones lose a little color and don't stand as straight up. Also, I know the edges experience greatest airflow and plants are usually quicker to dry out than those in the middle of the table. The bigger plants, that I can tell are more rooted, will dry out faster. Smaller and struggling plants with less established root systems can last up to three times as long without watering.

"The greenhouse also gets checked three times a day. For the tomatoes, unless it's morning on a hot sunny day, I only water the wilty plants and edges at each check. If they wilt between checks, water comes to their salvation before they get too stressed. Just be careful with this technique, because certain plants will not recover from even a mild wilt. Also, a plant that is producing fruit may react better or worse to the absence of water. The tolerance of different plants to drying out takes time to get a comprehensive understanding, but it only takes one wilty tomato dying for you to recognize and prevent future losses. Every plant has different needs and it's an art and science to be accurately attuned."

Kyros was so impressed and thankful for the information. "Where did you learn all of this, Garrett?"

"From Palo and the plants."

Palo came into the greenhouse to check on the progress and was pleased to see the day's plantings complete. Palo asked Kyros if he would like to help gather lunch.

When Palo shifted the cart into park, Kyros was trying to imagine what they could possibly eat that was growing near the pond. "Do you have a garden down here by the pond too?"

"Remember, my friend, just about everything growing is basically a garden of some form. While I plant and intervene to an extent with the land, I let most of nature's rhythms flow freely. We are going to try our luck at some crappie out of this pond as well as look for some early greens in the sunny areas."

They all grabbed a rod. Each was set up with a different artificial lure and casted into the clear waters. Immediately, Joel had a fish on the line. He pulled the hook from its mouth and showed Kyros that it was a bluegill and wasn't what they were after. He tossed it back as Kyros hooked into something a bit bigger. The reel whistled and the fish swam deeper into the water. A few minutes later the speckled side of a crappie flashed briefly.

Joel was impressed, shouting, "Did you see that thing?"

Palo rushed over and grabbed the net. "That guy's gotta be over a foot!"

Kyros eased the fish closer to shore. The fish spit the lure as Kyros pulled its head out of the water, but luckily Palo already had the net in place. The escapee retreated right into the floating mesh. The angler was ecstatic. "Ooh that guy's gonna taste so good."

Palo picked up the massive crappie. "I don't know. This one's one of the biggest I've ever seen in this pond. As nice as it would be to eat this fish, we need to let it go. This fish is too special to wind up for lunch." Palo handed the fish to Kyros to return to the water. The fish darted from his fingers and Palo murmured, "Bless you, my friend. Be strong on your journey. Thank you."

Kyros was taken back that he had just witnessed Palo bless and thank a fish that he let go. It didn't make sense. Before a question could even be put into words, Palo spoke. "The fish is a blessing to have caught and we are coming into its home to take some of its family for nourishment and sustenance. While the pond is part of our home too, we don't live, eat and breathe in her waters. It is our way of showing respect to the pond and all inhabitants and processes unfolding under her waters that we can only begin to understand. We don't own the life in the pond nor are we given the right to take and use whatever we want. If you listen to nature, she will tell you if you need to keep or release the fish. You will hear it in your heart."

The three returned to fishing. If Palo were to have spoken, he would've said the pond was happy, because within the next few minutes, four crappies were landed and placed in a bucket of water. Palo pulled a jar out of his pocket and sprinkled something green onto the ground, burnt some juniper and prepared to gut the fish on a flat rock with a hand-knapped piece of rainbow obsidian. Palo told Kyros that the knife had been gifted to him by a man who harvested it himself from the earth. The man had taught himself flint knapping and began making beautiful and powerful knives. Palo's shimmered in the sun like a technicolored fish.

Palo quickly stunned the fish with a rock and started working them with the precision of a heart surgeon. In no time, eight beautiful fillets were clean. The fillets were put into a clay vessel and the remaining carcasses into another. Both vessels were placed into a large clay pot in the back of the cart. Kyros was impressed and very inspired to see ice inside the larger clay pot. Palo had made the pots several years ago and used them as coolers.

With the fish in the cart, the team began searching the ground for greens. There weren't many, but after about ten minutes, Palo approached Kyros holding a handful of leaves. Kyros was shocked. "Those are dandelions. You can eat those?"

Palo gave one of his usual responses to these types of questions. He shifted his posture and smiled. "Most of the nuisance weeds that are sprayed with toxic chemicals in the quest to have perfect lawns are actually edible and highly medicinal. Those toxic chemicals are actually very harmful to the ecosystem, pets and children that play in the yards. Dandelions are one of the numerous wild foods and healers right in our front and back yards. They colonize undesirable, compacted and nutrient poor areas. Their growth and death importantly provide organic matter and they are some of the first plants involved with building up the soil. Also, they are an early food source before the growing season is in full swing as well as a source of pollen for bees when not much else has flowered. The roots and vegetative parts are all edible."

Kyros didn't know if this man was telling the truth, but his heart said he was. Kyros was starting to see the amount that he trusted Palo's knowledge, experience and expertise. Palo didn't have any degrees but was so credible. He had learned firsthand through direct experience the very lessons which he shared with Kyros, among others on a daily basis. He wasn't blindly governed by theory. He used theory, like the mind, as a great tool, but let experience lead, as with the heart. This seemed so valuable.

They gathered several ounces of dandelion greens, leaving the roots intact and undisturbed in the ground and drove up towards the house. They stopped in the meadow and harvested some spinach from the greenhouse. Joel explained that for spinach they use a cut and go method. When they plant, they seed it very close together. As it grows, the biggest leaves are harvested, in turn opening up the canopy for the slower growing plants to move in. This creates an easy system in which you plant once and harvest continually until the spinach bolts in the hotter months.

Joel pulled three large carrots out of the sandy soil outside the greenhouse. Kyros learned that they overwintered quite well under a thick layer of straw, leaves or other similar organic material. Kyros had never seen carrots that smelled or looked anywhere as good. They were red, yellow and purple – not even orange. Chives were cut at the base and about twenty radishes were harvested and placed into a basket with the carrots and spinach.

Palo walked back into the greenhouse to where there were two pots with potatoes growing. He reached straight into the black soil and pulled out five beautiful blue potatoes one after the other.

Abundant lighting in the family's kitchen gave the feeling of being as much outside as in. Dozens of plants filled the large open room that made up the living room, dining room, kitchen and entertainment room, with the stone fireplace in the middle - the altar of the medicine wheel. Vines hung in pots and draped down from the sky. Plants on the stairway going up to a bedroom climbed along the banisters. One of the bigger vines had must've had over fifty flowers stretching across a wall.

Palo told Kyros that it was tradition in the household for visitors to say or place a token of gratitude to the land on the stone altar built into the hearth of the fireplace. Kyros placed a rock that he'd picked up the first day he walked up Maya Bonita Creek, over the hill to the river and meadow. Every morning since, along with his glasses, the ordinary rock was delicately lifted from the nightstand and placed into a pocket. He thanked the land and the family and placed the rock by several other small pebbles on a green rock. Palo let him know that that was the special serpentine rock from the West Coast and that it was the only one on the entire property. The rock was beautiful, smooth and glossy.

All the greens were rinsed, dried and mixed in a wooden bowl. Palo said, "I carved and burned this bowl from an old burl that I found in the mountains." He used his hands to toss the greens. Joel lit a fire in the wood burning stove and started to set the table. The fire got going and the matriarch walked in. Her presence was vastly more powerful than even Palo or Bacchus Sophos. So moving, that every man and women would look at her as she walked into a public space or gathering. She gracefully moved over to the stove while humming a lovely melody.

The two introduced themselves. She put the fish on a plank of alder in the oven with the blue potatoes.

Joel came back into the room with applesauce, walnuts, sun dried tomatoes, dried peaches and honey from the root cellar. All of which they grew and prepared themselves within the food forest. He also had goat cheese that they made with the morning milk from their goat and homemade apricot vinegar.

He explained that goat cheese can be made in less than twenty minutes and seasoned with any combination of wet or dry ingredients you could think of. "We slowly bring the raw milk to a boil, continually stirring. Once boiling, we slowly add vinegar and keep stirring until it curdles. Then, we remove the pot from the heat and strain, using either a cheese cloth or a fine metal strainer. The clumps are cheese and the liquid that is left over is the whey. Some people leave different amounts of whey with the cheese, but I usually strain it out by pushing a plate over the cheese in the strainer. At this point you can season the cheese or put it in the fridge and season when you use it. It'll last about a week and a half to two weeks before it starts getting goaty."

Jacob Yastrow

A light concoction of vinegar, honey, a pinch of salt and frozen blackberries from the previous August were added, and the salad was tossed. Five hand carved wooden bowls that Kyros also presumed were from the land were filled with salad, and fillets of fish were removed from the oven and placed on top.

Joel's mother opened one of the upper cabinets and grabbed a jar labeled "Digestive Helper." Whistles sputtered from the tea kettle. In the last second before the cabinet shut, Kyros got a glimpse of just some of her herbs that she had grown, harvested, prepared and dried from the hundred and thirty acres. What he did see were dozens of half gallon jars neatly labeled and stacked full of different colored and textured plant medicine. She was an herbalist.

Joel put the bowls and tea on the table. The others followed. Each was given a soft fuzzy napkin woven with fibers from their alpacas. Kyros was about to dig in but realized the other three males were looking to the female. They were waiting for her to bless the meal.

She said, "Bless this food and the hands that made it. Bless the farmers that grew it and bless the fisherman who caught the fish. Bless the water, bless our bellies and bless the land. Bless the sun and the earth. Bless the plants and fish that allowed this meal. May this food nourish us and be a blessing of abundance. Bless myself, my husband, Palo and our son, Joel, who is my sun. Bless Garrett and his hard-working hands and loving heart. Bless our guest and friend, Kyros. Bless our home and bless our lives. Thank you all. We love and appreciate having the sustenance."

Everyone ate except for Kyros. He had heard grace and blessings before meals in the past, but it was always religious and slightly off-putting. He had never considered that the meal and the ones eating the meal could be blessed in a way that wasn't tied to Christ. Blessing in such a way gave a deep sense of connection and gratitude towards the food and the extended family. Even the sun was acknowledged.

Kyros put both hands around his bowl and closed his eyes for a second. He said to himself, "Bless this food and thank you plants and fishies for nourishing me," and took a bite.

He couldn't get over the fact that he helped harvest and prepare this bountiful meal from the land. Not to mention, he helped catch the fish this very morning. Garrett and Kyros joined Joel and his parents in meal, laughter and conversation. They all existed in a harmonious union so different than the usual meal that Kyros shared with his blood family. This was a different family and they contributed to the conversation and the experience as equals. Everyone's voices, minds and hearts were all valued and seen as much as anyone else's at the table.

After the meal, Kyros thanked his recently acquainted family for the unique experience to eat from the land. It was an experience foreign to Kyros, but everyday life for Garrett and Joel's family. Palo let Kyros know that he hoped to be in touch if Kyros was near or far after graduation and that he could always come back to the food forest to work for food any time he'd like.

When Kyros set his plate in the sink he didn't see the sharp chef knife in the soapy water. The knife sliced deep into the pad of his hand beneath his left thumb. Blood dripped from his wet hand into the sink. The soapy water turned a faint red within a few seconds. He started to panic.

The mother rushed over and immediately knew what to do. The wound needed attention. She needed to staunch it. She grabbed the powdered cayenne pepper and dumped half the bottle into the inch-long gash. Blood flow stopped right away. A minute later, she had gone into the Medicine Wheel Garden and returned with some herbs. She held them up to Kyros and said, "Chew these up, but don't swallow. I want to make a poultice out of yarrow and plantain."

Kyros complied. Once he chewed for several seconds, she held her hand in front of his mouth a few inches away. "Spit it out."

The green slobbery mush looked more like vomit than medicine. She pinched it into a small chunk, rinsed off the cayenne, at which point blood started flowing a little. She stuffed the chewed plants into the wound, applied more cayenne, followed by a few whole plantain leaves and wrapped his entire hand with a clean towel woven from one of their sheep.

She instructed that Kyros return in a couple days for her to look at it, and that he should pull off the bandage before bed and rinse out the wound. "Make sure to have cayenne by your side. I don't think it will bleed more, but it is fine if it does. Add some cayenne and it will stop. Rinse it out again tomorrow morning and evening. Make sure you let it breathe without any bandages after this evening. You can keep the towel as a gift. On Monday, you can come over after school so I can make sure you don't need anything more." She grabbed a jar out of the cabinet labeled "Organically Grown Cayenne Pepper" and filled a smaller container.

Kyros was still a little panicky so she gave him a few drops of a tincture. Within a minute he felt calm and relaxed, but not sedated. He drove home and followed her instructions over the next couple of days.

When he returned the wound was looking significantly better. She put a few drops of Saint John's Wort Oil into the healing cut and gave him his own bottle to take on his way. Her only instructions were to "Wash regularly. Each time, dry your hands thoroughly and apply a few drops into the cut just like I did. If you are worried about the rate or way it is healing after a week, then come back." She knew that he wouldn't need to come back. She had remedied countless cuts on herself, her family and her guests in a similar protocol.

The results were incredible and Kyros couldn't believe the power of the plants. He had got smaller cuts on his fingers that took twice as long to heal. With the oil, Kyros watched his wound close before his eyes. Within two weeks all that was left was a three-quarter inch scar.

Kyros reflected different paradigm shifts that he had experienced over the last several months. Bacchus Sophos, Demeter, Apollo, Zeus and Planao defied his expectations, giving him a new scope, which led to altered feelings and opinions about and towards homeless and transient individuals. Less meat was eaten and intentions were set to have a lifestyle that used less water. The food forest opened his eyes to a new way to feed the world and perceive wetlands.

When his hand healed in less than two weeks, his sole faith and support to Western modern medicine grew less faithful. For the first time, he truly and honestly believed eastern medicine held just as much value, if not more, as the value of modern hospitals, antibiotics and other branches of conventionally accepted health care in the country. He was baffled that health care provided nowhere near comparable coverage for other branches of less conventional treatments for his father with debilitating Multiple Sclerosis as modern Western treatments. Yoga, herbalists, naturopathic doctors, medicines and supplements had zero coverage or reimbursement from the insurance packages provided by his work. The acupuncturists that were covered were few and far between.

He pulled out his phone and wrote a poem about opinions.

Media, friends and family start one off

Without these influences opinion is lost

They help give a basis or a foundation to life

Molding perspectives morals support are right

A rock altered by the effects of erosion

The brain transforms from constant exposure

With knowledge drawn into the space between our ears

Alteration of perception begins to appear

Thoughts and theories on universal phenomena

Become more developed with reasoning to back them up

This creates individuals who do and believe as they please

Instead of people being brainwashed by the hierarchy

Jacob Yastrow

The Unexpected Invitation

School kept Kyros from the food forest as homework and final assignment due dates grew near. He became closer with Joel and would regularly trade twenty dollars for an assortment of root veggies and leafy greens from the land. Joel would share his wealth of knowledge on growing techniques and problem-solving shortcuts for different plant issues. Kyros learned powdery mildew could be taken care of by spraying baking soda and water on the foliage at dawn and dusk, but not in the middle of the day, for it can burn and stress the plants.

Kyros grew fascinated by a type of garden bed from Europe known as a Hügelkultur. Joel shared, "Our beds are self-tilling, watering, fertilizing and they generate heat from the decomposing logs and organic matter. We dig long trenches a few feet wide and about six inches deep and bury tree trunks, limbs and leaves in the original dirt. Then we mix our compost and more soil to put on top. Some people have a specific recipe for the layers involving sod placed upside down, but our way still works all the same.

"As the logs break down, they draw in moisture like a sponge. Snowmelt and spring and summer rains enter the soil, but don't drain out. It soaks into the logs, providing water in the hottest parts of the year. The breakdown of organic matter generates heat, and the snow never lasts long, especially on the south facing sides. You would be amazed how many more growing days a year we get on the Hügelkultur compared to our other outdoor beds. The decomposition also releases nutrients and aerates the soil, eliminating the need for tilling or fertilizing."

One day Joel brought an assortment of cooking and eating utensils that he unrolled from a beautiful brown and white piece of cow hide that the family had butchered and tanned themselves. The piece of leather continued turning over on the lunch table revealing spoon after fork after knife. Thirty-seven unique pieces that he hand-carved from an old peach tree sat in front of Kyros who was speechless. The creations from his sixteen-year-old classmate were exquisite.

As an early graduation present, Joel generously gifted Kyros a basic primitive mess kit with a deep wooden plate that could also serve as a bowl, along with a spatula, stirring spoon/ladle, fork, spoon and knife, which all fit neatly into the plate. The plate and everything inside came wrapped in a beautiful homemade leather pouch.

When Joel showed Kyros the pictures of the sprouted seeds that he planted and the young lettuce plants in the field, Kyros didn't believe that the seeds he planted survived. There were photos of plants growing in every cell. The lettuce was a mixture of reds and greens. The squash had grown so big that the cells were no longer visible.

On the last day of classes before finals week, Mr. Desert leaned over a put his arm on Kyros' desk. "Have you ever traveled out to Northern California?"

Kyros looked up from his notes, "San Francisco."

Green chuckled, "Any further?"

"No, why?"

"There are trees over three times the size of the trees that used to grow at the Maya Bonita natural area and there are hundreds of travelers, like Planao and my other friends, that are considered homeless, yet everywhere they go they feel home."

"Three times the size?" Kyros thought Green had to be joking. He also didn't know that his teacher knew about the mismanaged landscape on the edge of town.

The instructor pulled out a picture of himself standing next to the trunk of a tree that was easily three times wider than his outstretched arm span. It was a picture that sat amongst the other twenty-five tree pictures in Green's office.

Kyros asked, "Where is this?"

"Green exclaimed, "Northern California!"

"That sounds like a sweet offer, but I have no money. Also, I don't think my parents will let me."

"Kyros, your only major expense will be food. I plan to hitchhike, and I even have an extra sleeping bag that you can take."

"Oh no. There's no way in hell my mom is going to let me hitchhike halfway across the country."

"Well, when do you turn eighteen? Would it be so bad for you to tell them I was driving?"

"June, and I don't know."

"Perfect, I'll wait to leave until June, and I will let you ask them however you'd like."

Kyros feared bringing up the subject at dinner that night. He made the move while his mom cleared the table. "Mom, Dad…one of my teachers invited me to travel with him this summer. He wants to drive out West and I really want to see the trees."

"No." The room fell silent. His mother spoke again several tense seconds later. "You want to see the trees?"

Kyros felt so small. He thought for a moment and made the connection that the redwoods on the notebook in the greenhouse were the same species of tree in the same state that Green stood in front of in the picture. Nothing made sense in his head, but he remembered his lesson from Palo and knew that he was going to let his heart guide him to Northern California, regardless if his family wanted him to. He hit his fists on the table and stood up. "Well, I'm going to be eighteen and you can't stop me."

His dad's fork hit the table and his napkin landed on the floor. The father looked sternly into his son's eyes and questioned, "With what money do you intend on spending to get you out of any trouble, let alone on food or gas?"

"I have a few hundred saved up." His parents both erupted with laughter. To them, it was inconceivable to last off a few hundred dollars for the summer.

His mom wiped a tear from her eye, "You couldn't last a month on that much money."

Kyros thought his mom was right and grew discouraged, but he refused to let it show. He pushed his chair in. "I'm going up to my room and I am going to go whether you like it or not."

Thirty seconds later the bedroom door slammed and Kyros flung himself onto the bed, tears streaming down cheeks and face in hands. Between snobs and snot, sense started to return. The reason, hazy, for such a negative reaction to his parents' dismissal. Compelled to travel with his teacher to the West Coast, an internal fire flickered. Was it the redwoods or was it the transient people?

The fact of the matter was the wind was guiding him. Although his mind was clouded in fog, Kyros felt a calling in his heart and a visit to the redwoods seemed like a much greater accomplishment and success than going to college. Traveling lightly in unfamiliar territory without any commitments or obligations was vastly more fulfilling than getting a mindless job for a company that didn't fully see or value him. He was starting to see that his worth was so much more than any summer job. He had heard stories of people hitchhiking across the country or riding trains and figured he could get himself back in two to three months regardless how bad things got.

The following morning his mom made the announcement. "Honey, we've decided to support you and let you leave on your trip. We want you to be well off on your travels, so your father and I have decided to give you one thousand dollars as a graduation present. Your phone and car insurance will be cancelled, but don't take that as a reason to not stay in touch. If anything goes wrong, just call. We love you and we want you to be safe and happy. When you run out of money, we will pay to get you back and you can once again join the real world by becoming a productive member of society." Kyros rushed over and gave her a hug while repeatedly thanking her.

Humboldt County

One of Green's friends dropped the two intrepid travelers off at a gas station one block from the onramp. They grabbed a few snacks and drinks, used the bathroom and walked towards the interstate.

Hitchhiking was illegal, but that was less of a concern to Kyros than the scenario of getting picked up by someone dangerous. Thinking about the situation warranted an uncomfortable chuckle. As the driver, every hitchhiker's intentions and background got questioned, but now that he was about to hold up a sign himself, the roles were reversed. Half a block from the highway Kyros started to look for anything wrong with the situation.

Green politely calmed and encouraged him, offering compassion and said, "Please, think if you have any reasons from the heart that aren't based in fear or anxiety as to why this isn't a good idea." Kyros could think of none.

Green looked to Kyros again. Cars accelerated past them onto the interstate. He said, "You are going to encounter some educational and emotional experiences, fair warning. Stay strong. They are all part of the journey. From here on out I want you to think of me not as your teacher, Mr. Desert, but as a friend, Green. We are both on a journey of self-discovery. "

Kyros was confused. "But I'm only about to turn eighteen and I don't even know how old you are."

"My friend, age is a concept based on a perception someone had somewhere at some time. If we abide by the perceptions instilled by people, then our reality will be as such. I don't want you to ever forget what I have pieced together in my head that I'm about to share.

"Perception is reality. It doesn't matter if the creator of the perception knows it's not true, the illusions that are received by the listener or audience become their truth and reality…" Green paused for impact. "…if the listener or audience lets it."

Green giggled to himself. "Your reality of age is based on a commonly accepted perspective, but I have seen through the illusion and know time is an abstract concept. Our lives play out in the equivalent of days for mighty redwoods, yet our days are years to other creatures. Time and age compartmentalize our very being.

"Institutions and our society love compartmentalization, because it allows order and control. Locations of the sun, moon and stars relative to the horizon are sufficient aids in coordinating our lives with other humans and beings at a set time and date.

"From what I've put together, it is frequently best to avoid compartmentalization. The word implies to put into a defined space so a target can be contained. It implies that a human of your age must only do what is expected by that age label. Don't let labels dictate reality. The description of the compartmentalized label is also such that you can't act according to the next successive compartment until you've fulfilled duties and objectives of the current. It goes the same for the previous compartments, labels and levels.

"Once completed, it isn't optimal for the institution to have individuals return to a previous level or compartment. What would happen if every twenty to forty-year-old paying rent in Silicon Valley decided to go live with their moms to generate a savings account instead of paying upwards of four thousand dollars a month to rent a studio as large as my classroom at the school?

"With this paradigm, me being friends with you – a member of a much prior compartment – is perceived as unorthodox by the people who are defined by this very way of thought. Does that make sense?"

Kyros responded, "I think so. So basically, you're saying to let actions disprove labels instead of labels constituting actions."

"Well said, man." Green Desert took off his shirt. He looked more like a hippy at a festival than a high school teacher. Green handed Kyros a poem. The paper was old and faded. Green said, "I wrote this a few years back."

One of the spiritual

My place of prayer isn't a synagogue or church

Always a student

My classroom isn't in a university or college

Forever a warrior

Far from guns and the Middle East

Not a businessman

I strive for virtue and value, not for money and success

Not a physicist

Yet starting to grasp the gravity of the neglect of nature and fellow man

A man of facts

Standing behind the evidence

A man of faith

Confidently approaching desired path

On a quest for truth

I know it's self-perceived and different for me and each of

you

A man of science

A man of art

A man of passion

A man of peace

A man of spirit

A man of wonder

A man of earth

A man of me

Green repeated Kyros' words shortly after the poem was recited. "Let actions disprove labels instead of labels constituting actions. I learned that from a wise man and friend." The two laughed, Kyros felt the statement was a good joke, yet Green truly believed and meant what he said.

From the cab Green and Kyros watched the road wind through mountains along Highway 299 from Redding. The truck driver was explaining that Northern California was home to the tallest trees on earth. He talked about the thick coastal fog that provided enough water for the redwood trees to soar above all else. As the coast drew nearer, the clouds thickened, the humidity rose and the trees grew. The 299 met up with the Mad River and the smell of pot filled the air.

Kyros couldn't believe that they had just hitchhiked across half of the continent and were now zigzagging along a breathtaking canyon above an emerald river. He had heard so much about the Rocky Mountains of Colorado, yet this was easily as stunning as the Colorado interstate that climbed up and down mountains into Utah.

It had been a week since his mom had seen him and his teacher hitchhiking on the north end of town. She had been on her way to work, presuming the two were driving out west in a vehicle, and made direct eye contact with Kyros as she turned towards the onramp. By the time she registered what happened, the car was already accelerating onto the highway. It wasn't possible to back up or immediately turn around.

Kyros didn't know, but she had turned around and by the time she got there eight minutes later, the two hitchhikers had already been picked up and were heading west through the plains, towards the mountains.

It had taken five days and four frigid nights to get to Salt Lake City, then on the morning of the sixth they managed to catch a lucky ride all the way to Redding. Fifteen hours later they were camping on the shores of Whiskeytown Reservoir.

The temperature couldn't have been cooler than fifty degrees Fahrenheit. The location was easily the most remote place Kyros had ever stayed the night. They possessed only what him and Green could carry.

Both men were exhausted and had less than a dozen hours of sleep in the last few nights. Not to mention they had just traveled over a thousand miles in one day in a stranger's car. The driver was going into the Trinity Alps and could only take the two as far as the recreation area.

In the darkness of the night, Kyros held a flashlight in his mouth. Green wore a dim headlamp which died halfway down the mountain.

Kyros slid down the rocky hillside on his butt with backpack in one hand and their water in the other. Both were so heavy that the contents were on the verge of slipping from his hands upon making it down the fifty-foot slide. His legs were a little cut up, but Green was in worse shape. The man was sitting blind in a clump of manzanitas with his backpack tangled above that held their food, stove and cooking supplies.

Kyros shined his light up the hill saw Green struggling to escape from the pokey shrubs. His backpack, hair and clothes were all intertwined.

A few minutes later Kyros had scrambled back up the hill. The young adult had to slide down and grab Green's pack without getting stuck himself. The trapped teacher picked the worst route.

A few feet before the jumble of plants and human, Kyros was able to stop himself by grabbing ahold of a root sticking out of the mountainside. He had to slide slowly down the root, which was unknown if alive, without ripping it from the earth. Green was situated below the pack that stopped falling before he did.

At this point, both individuals were acclimated enough to see in the dark. A combined effort of Green pushing, and Kyros twisting and pulling, freed the pack. After a few more painful minutes, Green freed himself from the manzanitas and was sitting next to Kyros. They were both so tired and still had to collectively scoot twenty feet across the face of the hill and slide into camp without dropping the pack.

Thirty minutes after the ordeal began, the two were both safely on the flat with no major injuries or mishaps with supplies – only some scrapes deep enough to draw blood. Luckily, Kyros still had his Saint John's Wort oil. Neither could exert much more energy for the night. They both ate a granola bar and a slice of leftover pizza, before pulling out their sleeping bags. They fell asleep at two in the morning under the stars.

Around eight in the morning they were awoken by a brigade of motorcycles at least seventy strong. Tired and sore, the two men packed up their sleeping bags and struggled to make it back to the highway where they were picked up by the first passing truck.

Once in Arcata, they relaxed in the plaza for a few hours. Midafternoon they headed uphill into the community forest with their loaded-up packs. The dry season was beginning, but the ground was still damp. They joined a group of transient voyagers and entered into a time turning land. It looked to Kyros like they were venturing into prehistoric realms. Redwoods and four-foot-tall Sword Ferns grew everywhere. Nowhere else that he had ever been seemed more fitting for a dinosaur to appear.

Once camp was set up in the steep valley, dozens of people gathered in a circle and everyone started rolling joints and packing pipes. Kyros had never smoked before.

Jacob Yastrow

For a couple hours the group proceeded to get higher. Kyros' mind grew hazy, but he began to analyze every word and action differently. Perception and perspective in his stoned state made him question everything that he had ever known. He saw the individuals in the circle not as homeless, but as travelers on their own journeys. Filthy and wearing tattered clothes, everyone besides Green and himself had abandoned the conventional material world and owned only what they could carry. What they lacked in possessions, they made up for in experience and a connection to mother earth.

This train of thought paused. Never had Kyros perceived the earth as a female or even a living entity. He remembered the natural area near Maya Bonita Creek and the similar connection he felt when roaming the landscape before stumbling across the trash and the massive tree trunks.

Coincidently, Kyros looked past a few of the people to see trash scattered about at the base of tree stumps greatly exceeding the ones from back home. The redwoods still standing were up to five feet in diameter, but some of the
120

stumps were nearly twenty. There were a few even larger. Kyros looked to the vagabond to his left and asked, "What happened to those trees?" He pointed across the circle.

The man's smile faded, and his head drooped. "The redwoods are highly valued for their rot and fire-resistant wood. When they were first uncovered by white man, they started to fall one by one. More people arrived and more got cut. Large tracts of pristine virgin forest were clear-cut, which destroyed the whole ecosystem from trees to animals to the soil. These redwoods you see today are second or third growth, but the old growth forests have been nearly lost entirely."

"Old growth?"

"Yes. Once a forest reaches a certain age with trees of a certain size, it becomes an old growth forest. All ecosystems have different ages that scientists will classify as old growth. Commonly, they are areas that have never been logged. These ecosystems are the most resilient and structurally diverse with trees of all sizes. The forest you see now is unstable, less healthy and less productive, with trees that max around eighty or one hundred and twenty years old. Only about five percent of old growth Coastal Redwood forests still remain. You mustn't leave this pocket of the country until you explore those remaining forests of giants. The trees here might be a buck-fifty tall, but the tallest redwoods exceed three hundred and fifty feet."

Trees of that size seemed unfathomable to Kyros and he pleaded to know where to find these ancient treasures. The man pulled out a map and made several circles.

Kyros anticipated seeing the colossal trees. As the day grew closer the young man spent more time traveling around and learning about the instability and degradation of the local ecosystems. One morning he walked alone on the beach and came across a group of people huddled around a large object. He approached and realized that it was a whale. He waited until a woman paused and inquired what had happened. As Kyros looked closer, he noticed that the whale's fins were pinned against its body, constricted. "Did the net kill this creature?" The whale was easily forty feet long.

The instructor responded, "This Grey Whale likely swam into the net in the last couple weeks and has been dead for maybe three days." The smell was awful and when the wind stopped blowing a few students gagged. One threw up their lunch. All was silent except the seagulls, the wind and the waves.

Kyros thanked the teacher and walked away with the image of the entangled whale a branded memory. That whale was easily the most impressive animal that he had ever seen.

For a couple hours he walked, trying to rationalize a solution or common ground to balance the need to feed people and the need to protect species like the Grey Whale that died trapped in a drift net. He wasn't sure if people could be fed from the ocean without any nets – only fishing line and crab pots. He had even seen places growing up where fishing line threatened wildlife like pelicans. It didn't seem possible for everyone in America to be sustained and nourished from properties like Palo's food forest. Could people be sustained and thrive without

Jacob Yastrow

food insecurities via small-scale, sustainable, diversified, regenerative and holistic agricultural practices?

In the afternoon, Kyros went for a hike near the town of Trinidad to Strawberry Rock. All the redwoods were relatively small and Kyros could tell their age was young. After about fifteen minutes he noticed two larger redwoods growing about ten feet apart. A noise in the canopy caught his attention. Upon craning his neck upward, he noticed two platforms over sixty feet in the air. A rope with a carabiner bridged the gap for safety. A tree-to-tree jump was manageable for the brave. The main shelter in the left was no more than ten feet square and the wooden landing in the right was even smaller. Pots, shoes and other belongings hung from the floor, dangling five-stories above Kyros and the ferns. Walls and roof were tarps.

Further up the trail a sign that stretched between another two trees read, "STOP CLEARCUTTING". A man caught up to Kyros and spoke of the tree sits. "People live in the trees to prevent them from being logged. Clear-cutting is a practice where every tree is cut in an area leaving only

124

stumps and barren mountains." Kyros looked again at the
sign thirty-five feet overhead. The words were bold and
stood out against the background of the banner. "STOP
CLEARCUTTING". Every tree in the image was cut with
dozens of stumps remaining. The scene barren and closer
resembling a war zone post detonation than a lush forest
like the one he was standing amidst. On the ground the
landscape looked healthy like the community forest in
Arcata, but Kyros started to piece the situation together.

The parking area was a dead-end street at a gate marked
"PRIVATE PROPERTY" and the only reason Kyros pressed
on was because the group in front of him didn't seem the
slightest bit perturbed. There were also twelve cars
parked. All around, the land had been clear-cut and he
could see it. Huge stumps, like those in the community
forest, lingered in the valley. Even though the forest looked
lush, not too many years ago it had been clear-cut and
would've looked like the desolate wasteland pictured on
the banner. Kyros hadn't yet seen the old growth forests
and didn't quite understand how clear-cutting could be so
bad if the landscape regenerated a few decades later. He

realized that the community forest must've been clear-cut too, yet it was the greenest landscape he had ever seen.

The man introduced himself and elaborated on tree sits. "Some have sat for years and it has proven to be a radical, yet effective civilian conservation measure. The first sits happened decades ago to protect the old growth. These are the largest trees for miles. Loggers used to kill protesters who opposed their indiscriminate massacre on privately owned property that was never theirs, and the cops would watch. Trees would be felled next to those who would refuse to come down and face charges and the very trunks of trees that people sat in would be rammed as an intimidation tactic or to just seek vengeance. There were even cases of helicopters flying in close proximity to tree sitters, forcing them to hold on for dear life. If they didn't hold on, they would've plummeted to the forest floor."

Appalled and disgusted, Kyros couldn't believe what this earnest man was saying, but then he could. This wasn't an isolated instance of the assault and harassment of those who were only asking to value and protect the land. Reflections of Standing Rock struck a similar dissonant cord. A society that allowed for pipelines across sacred land and the largest water table in the United States had been governed and influenced by the same values which allowed old growth forests to be decimated on global and local levels.

When Kyros and his family took a trip to The Badlands and Mount Rushmore they observed two white men spit in the face of a Lakota women, while a Sheriff and police officer watched. The cops, implicated to uphold the law and private property rights, legally couldn't do anything. In another instance they watched 911 get called on a warm Lakota family for eating in a privately owned establishment on the sad basis of them being "Indian."

At the top of the hill the trees thinned. Soon they came across a large quarry. The earth dug up with no trees at all. The sight was disturbing, the devastation angering.

On top of the rock, Kyros could see young forest all the way to the ocean. He turned to see a cleared, barren ridgeline.

The man spoke again. "That big chunk that's gone is a clear-cut. They come in with their machines and cut down every tree. You see, the land is destroyed and all that remains are bald hills and mountaintops that regrow in the same twenty-acre fragments that are rotationally cut. Many native species can't exist. They get overrun and outcompeted by invasive species. Soil would normally be held in place by the roots of trees. Without the topsoil, the earth erodes and clogs the arteries and veins, the lifeblood of the land. Erosion and other factors have contributed to the decline of the salmon, steelhead and lampreys.

"My ancestors and their decedents have lived in this land for some time now, but our way of life has been more and more jeopardized. The Klamath River used to have thousands of miles of flow and tributaries, but now several dams keep salmon from their upstream spawning grounds. When salmon cannot pass, they die without reproducing. The next generation lost. Dams also limit water flow, causing shallower, warmer and slower rivers. Often not enough water flows for the fish to travel. In slower and warmer waters, toxic algae thrive and create anaerobic conditions. The salmon are disappearing, and we don't know how we will survive."

Kyros was taken back. "What happens to the water?"

The Native American attending the local university sniffled. His voice trembled. "Some is stored for recreation or to provide water for people, but most goes to lands where it never was meant to flow. Big agriculture is stealing our water."

This talk on dams was a paradox to Kyros. He learned in school that dams were good and provided a clean source of renewable energy. Now this stranger on a sacred landmark was telling him that dams were a very large contributing factor to the decline of fish populations. It didn't make sense why people would be growing food in the Central Valley if there wasn't water. This was all so much for Kyros to take in.

Everything he thought he knew a year ago was wrong. His world was turning upside down and he started getting an immense headache that felt like someone was pulling his hairs straight out. So many memories and thoughts about significant past events occupied his mind. The man pulled out a guitar and started playing to the sunset. Kyros pulled out his phone and wrote a poem.

I know a man who has a lot on his mind, he doesn't know what to do
So many things that he thinks about, it clouds his mind
Every day so many thoughts on his plate he contemplates conversation
Where is his place? What fate will he face? How he'll give to the world?

He sings, "Oh, I'll keep going until the end of my world
Oh, I'll keep exploring towards places I can call home."

I know a man who's ambitious as can be, all it takes is knowing what he seeks
He just has to convince himself first it will help fulfill dreams
So many people in a world with so many problems that generations are now taught to solve

Within our relations there aren't enough equations

Solutions allow formulae to be resolved

We sing, "Oh, I'll keep going until the end of my world

Oh, I'll keep exploring towards places I can call my home."

The sun got lower on the horizon. The ocean stretched for eternity. Kyros wrote another poem.

Creeping through the valley

Riverside

Looking for something to light our minds

A search for reason

A guiding source

A melody heard amongst the noise

I came here to this river

to this place of spirit to collect myself

I came here to water flowing over rocks

to this place of spirit to collect myself

before

Walking through the forest

Mountainside

I need those trees to ease my mind

A search for peace

A break from cities

So many folks have peculiar priorities

I came here to this mountainside

to this place of spirit to collect myself

I came here to trees growing out of the earth

to this place of spirit to collect myself

Sitting on a rock

Mountaintop

I need some time alone with my thoughts

A search for solace

I want to find my way

Maybe I'll know where I'm heading one of these days

I came here to this mountaintop

to this place of spirit to collect myself

I came here to this rock on the earth

to this place of spirit to collect myself

Lying on the beach

Crash of waves

My mind in a haze

Rest for a while

I can still smile

Live carefree like a child

I came here to this foggy coast

to this place of spirit to collect myself

I came here to where ocean meets land in one hand

to this place of spirit to collect myself

The guitarist and Kyros hiked out in silence and rode the public transit back to Arcata.

Jacob Yastrow

Old Growth Forest

Kyros caught a ride the following morning up the coast.
From the back-seat window, the old growth redwoods on
the northeast shore of Big Lagoon were easily the biggest
he'd visited, and even these were tiny compared to what
he would soon encounter.

Entering Del Norte Coast Redwoods State Park further
north was one of the most powerful experiences of his life.
He stood among trees larger than any he ever anticipated.
Trees that started a couple hundred feet downhill still
towered above his head.

One specimen was so enormous that a car could've pulled
halfway into the blackened scar. Kyros walked over and
pressed his face against the moist, spongy wood that was

soft yet strong enough to support his weight. He gripped the red outer bark and looked into a cavity that extended more than fifty feet up the trunk. The air inside the cavity was dark and cooler than the air outside. There was no breeze. Charred into the trunk was a grid pattern that disappeared into the hollowed cathedral. His hands were stained black after stroking the pronounced lines. It didn't make sense. The tree had burned and the exposed surface resembled charcoal. The other trees were smaller and none showed any indication of such an even.

Kyros quickly tuned into the methodic timeline of the surrounding ecosystem. Patterns unfolded with nothing more than observation. The density of vegetation established on the fallen trees hinted at the order each must have fallen. The trunks that had begun their slow return to soil less recently had new trees growing over a hundred feet in the air. He would later learn that frequently the trees growing out of nurse logs were Western Hemlocks. One stood suspended above the ground like a mangrove revealing the roots that would've once grown around and through an ancient redwood that fell a thousand years ago or more.

The forest was blissful and quiet. Variation in the landscape existed, but the predominant plants were the same. Arching and crawling huckleberry and man-sized ferns cloaked the ground with sorrel filling in all the gaps. Like the food forest, this mature landscape showed little exposed soil.

He traversed a steep hillside before heading back towards the road. Near a small creek, he came across a couple smoking. He asked if he could join and took a seat. They shared their stories and asked if he'd ever been to Prairie Creek State Park. The wife spoke of other trees with massive caverns burned out of the trunks. It didn't take long for them to hook Kyros' attention and he graciously accepted an invitation for a ride that night.

At the campfire they brought out a couple guitars and a banjo. The three of them played late into the night. Kyros didn't think he was very skilled, but the music sounded so beautiful and enchanting. They played as equals, all contributing to the experience of musical expression. Like a radio, the trio were a receiver for the universe's frequencies.

Kyros departed at dawn and followed the trail markers to "Big Tree." Low angles of light beamed through the canopy as he stood on the wooden platform at her base. The trunk was the biggest he'd seen, and it grew in a strange matter with large snags. The original top had been broken, yet the tree was still alive, thriving and huge. A plaque indicated its circumference, diameter, height and estimated age. Over fifteen hundred years old and over two hundred-fifty feet tall, this was the biggest and oldest living creature he'd ever dreamed of. He pictured the tree much younger, growing through the changes of time, climate and cultures. This tree had experienced so much. It felt like the tree was wiser than any man as well as all of men collectively. A tree with so much to share and all Kyros had to do was sit there and take it in. He left humbled and at a loss for words. He had never felt such a connection to the earth.

Back at camp, the couple explained fire is often an integral part of the forest ecology and even the Coastal Redwoods possess advantageous traits to withstand periodic burns in intervals ranging from ten years to over five hundred years.

This came as shocking news, but a long return interval was the perfect explanation as to why only the oldest and biggest tree on the hillside showed remnants of the burn. Kyros always had been taught that fire was bad and a threat to lands.

The boyfriend went into detail about forest succession and how moderate disturbances create areas where new trees of different species can establish. Kyros then learned that a regular cycle of low to medium intensity fires help keep accumulated and flammable brush off the ground and reduce competition. The higher the frequency, the less there was to burn at ground level. He said, "The old growth redwood bark is actually fire resistant. In the event that the fire burns past this defensive shield…" the man walked over and rubbed the moist bark on a nearby giant, "…large cavities get scorched out of the inside, leaving what you have seen in the last couple of day. As long as the bark isn't burned around the entire trunk, the tree can persist for centuries after.

"Certain trees actually require fire to complete their life cycles. Some pine trees are serotinous, which means they need fire or intense heat to release their seeds. This is likely a survival mechanism to ensure there is no light or space competition for the seedling after sprouting.

"Oak woodlands are a specific type of habitat in which fires are crucial for their long-term existence. In California, these woodlands have grown increasingly less frequent over the last hundred and fifty years in response to fire suppression. When natural fire cycles are tampered with, Douglas-fir moves into the oak woodland and outcompetes the oaks for light. New oaks can't get established and old oaks get choked out. Oaks can withstand low to medium intensity fires, but the young Douglas-firs don't stand a chance. Historically the natives of this land would've had prescribed burns in the oak woodlands to ensure the security of a food crop."

Right when Kyros didn't think he could be more impressed by trees, especially the Coastal Redwoods, he picked up a small woody object from the ground near the campfire. "What's this?"

The girlfriend quickly responded. "It's a redwood cone."

Kyros held it up closer to his face. "This little thing? No way."

"It is! I know that it seems unrealistic that such tiny little cones come from the tallest trees in the world, but generally the longer lived a plant is, the less effort it puts to reproduction. A redwood might shed over a million cones in a lifetime, but very few will grow into the next generation. Many of the cones are duds, without seeds, which keeps birds and small animals from seeking them out as a general food source. Of the cones that do have viable seeds, they don't always germinate or grow. On the other hand, annuals generally have beautiful and vibrantly showy reproductive parts to ensure that their genetics remain part of the gene pool."

Kyros inspected the little crevasses of the cone for any seeds and found none.

He remembered the giant pinecones that lined the edge of the road before entering Humboldt County. One cone must've weighed as much as his head and was equally as large. The truck driver had told him and Green that the woody pinecones that they see are the female reproductive organ and bare seeds. The pollen cones are the male organ. Pollen is dispersed by the wind to the immature ovulate cones awaiting fertilization. The trucker stopped in a pull off to show them a stand of Ghost Pines he found the previous week. The cones were developing towards head-size and were rainbow colored and the size of his fists.

Kyros looked at the tiny redwood cone again and tossed it on the ground. He figured the Ghost Pines must not live anywhere near as long as redwoods.

Sitka Spruce

Redwoods were the only coastal tree species of interest until Kyros stumbled across a large Sitka Spruce with gray scaly bark. With the redwoods from Prairie Creek consuming his mind, the different species of trees and ultimately all the different groups of plants along the coast of Northern California would've remained unnoticed. That is until curiosity enticed the young man to walk down a road near the north end of Big Lagoon.

Light grew faint and the sounds of birds filled the air, while the noise of traffic lessened. Fast growing alders and young Douglas-firs crowded the path. At the end of the dense maze of trunks, Kyros entered a forest of a different kind of tree. The understory looked like the community forest, but the trees here gave an eerie but humbling

Jacob Yastrow

ambiance. The outer bark grew in a way that resembled square potato chips. The gray trunks flared at their bases and the mosses living on the spongy ground had colonized extensively up the trunks, blanketing the brittle wood.

One tree towered over a hundred feet into the air. He looked up and saw limbs teaming with life. Mosses, lichens, ferns and other plants covered the tops and sides of every branch. All Kyros could see were plants. Still riddled with the green blur, he had yet to learn to see the plants as individuals themselves and not just as part of the forest. In time he would learn how to identify ferns from huckleberries, Salmonberry from salal and *Pseudotsuga* from *Tsuga*. All he saw were plants growing on plants which were all growing on a tree with potato chip bark.

The bottom forty feet of lateral growth was all dead, with at least that much more alive above. The lowest branches stretched away from the column and disappeared into the ferns. Kyros started to feel very compelled to climb. It was an enormous tree by most standards, but still adolescent to the massive redwoods that he had experienced in the old

144

growth forests such as Big Tree. Nonetheless, this spruce was a force of its own and was easily the tallest on the hillside.

Kyros' first impressions of the unusual plants growing on the bark weren't much of one. A closer look revealed extraordinary alien-like creatures. Some were hard and crusty; some had little lobes and some hung pendant, lime green, dangling over five feet. The texture of others mimicked a soft, wet, shag carpet.

Kyros analyzed the diversity of lifeforms near the base before a climbing attempt. The first limb gave way under his right foot. The next one came loose under his left. Hoping branches would be stronger higher up, he extended both arms and grabbed two more about six and a half feet up. An equal distribution of weight between his two arms and his right leg on the trunk allowed him to pull and scurry up the tree until he was standing about fifteen feet up.

He looked down, then up and saw dead growth in both directions. There was enough lateral vegetation that it seemed unrealistic for death to come in response to error in judgement. If he were to fall from even forty feet, there would be over fifty chances for him to grab ahold of something, or at the very least, slow his fall on the way down. However, getting impaled by a broken stick was a very real threat.

Step by step he made his way toward the canopy. He paused on the first living branch to brush the insects from his body and the spider webs from his face. He managed to only break a handful of limbs. A thought from Palo popped into his head. Palo had grabbed a chunk of decomposing wood from a pile at the base of a dead tree in the food forest. He let out a chuckle, while smaller pieces crumbled out of his hands between his fingers and said, "All of these plants return to the soil." Kyros thought about the Sitka Spruce returning to soil too.

Four stories up, the tree was as lush as the forest floor. Water dripped down his back each time he reached up and grabbed the next branch. Grays, browns and a dozen shades of yellow and green created a beautiful mosaic of life. There were more species of plants in the canopy than the total number of tree species in the forest.

At the top, the breeze gently rocked him several feet. The soothing rhythm triggered Kyros to enter a trance. His mind drifted into deep thought. Though not scared, he felt strangely safe – more comfortable than in any city or classroom full of people. He loaded a pipe and took several hits. He breathed in at the same timing as the sway of the trunk. He pulled out his phone and began to write.

All his most powerful memories from the eye doctor to the old growth redwoods were held tight in his mind. So were the lessons from the hippies, the instructor on the beach, the man on Strawberry Rock, to Green, Bacchus Sophos and the other travelers on their own journeys. Kyros began to write a poem.

I sat in the crown of a towering tree
A monument of nature – surpassing surroundings
A few hundred years would be a safe bet

Jacob Yastrow

My mere eighteen felt so insignificant
Never have I ever felt so much one with nature
As a human - prime devastator
The annihilator - came and conquered
Not giving two fucks for the indigenous
Here I am in Humboldt County
In this new forest that has allowed me to see my calling

He wasn't certain how, but he once again had a strong inclination that he needed to be a light for the world. Another poem came forth and he pulled his phone back out of his pocket.

I keep the things I love in the back of my mind
I will try to live a life that's divine
Full of virtue and value
I hope it influences some of you

I try to be the change in the world I want to see
I believe I can see what the world needs to be

Less corporations and greed

Less things that scream tyranny while life seeks stability

Fight for the world once and for all

Fight for the world once and for all

Fight for the world once and for all

Fight for the world once and for all

He became more grounded with each foot on the descent. Unfortunately, more branches broke under his weight. A sharp pain arose in his heart. The discomfort grew more intense following the trampling of a fern at the base of the tree. The fallen limbs were scattered around the trunk like clockwork, all from him. To many, the act might not have had an impact, but Kyros purely and honestly held empathy for the forest and the powerful Sitka Spruce. He never wanted to climb a tree again if it meant breaking off branches that contained so much life.

Kyros spent a few weeks exploring the dramatic landscapes of the northern half of California and every day, with every thought and experience, became more displeased towards society. He learned the same plant he had smoked to expand his consciousness was causing major environmental problems. Excess fertilizers made it into streams which caused algal blooms. Fishers and wildlife were being poisoned from anticoagulant rodenticides. Streams were being diverted to supply water and forests were clear-cut. From Google Earth all the greenhouses and grows on mountain tops were evident.

He took a trip down south through the Central Valley. He saw the irrigated water that had been diverted from the northern watersheds through pipes and canals. He came across a pole roughly a hundred feet high with an informative sign at the base. The top of the pole indicated the ground level in the early part of the twentieth century. Due to countless wells that had been drilled, the ground had sunk about a hundred feet. The soil had become severely compacted and the aquifers had been nearly depleted. People were constantly drilling deeper. Many scientists and farmers feared the soil in the Central Valley may never recover. Once compacted, water could no longer properly enter the soil and percolate into the water table.

Kyros learned that the Central Valley used to be one of the largest wetlands in the nation until ditches, levees and monocultures replaced marshes, meandering rivers and wildlife. An old farmer at a market said, "There used to be water, but never enough for what the people would want. Hardly any water remains and the sun scorched desert can now only remember the lush wetlands that used to be." It seemed shocking that most of the produce grown in the United States was grown right in the Central Valley.

Days later, Kyros traveled by a large lake and saw an empty valley with next to no water. He thought about the reservoir back home, the kitchen sink, his steak dinner, the salmon, the pot grows, the historic wetlands in the Central Valley and the diverted water from the north. Places were running out of water. He felt people were taking more than they should. They were taking more than the land could give.

With his backpack on, Kyros walked through Yosemite Valley and onward. He slept amongst the most massive trees on the planet in Giant Sequoia National Park. Trash littered the popular trail and he spotted a crow defending a half-eaten pepperoni pizza that someone had left on a bench. This was a very special place and Kyros couldn't comprehend the moral and ethical dilemma of leaving food and trash behind.

Green departed back east shortly after Kyros returned. It was nearing the end of summer and a few weeks of preparation before fall semester was in order. Kyros was excited to experience the next leg of his life yet was sad to be leaving his beloved mentor and friend. They parted on good terms and had a strong feeling their paths would cross again. Kyros intended on taking a bus back east a few weeks later. His mother had reluctantly and conditionally accepted the desire to wait a semester before starting college, providing he immediately got a job or dedicated at least twenty hours a week to a skill or interest that could be used to support him.

Green gave Kyros a big hug and said, "Remember your truths. Listen to your heart but use your mind. You will do great things in this world. You are more capable than you or anyone else could ever imagine."

Jacob Yastrow

The Tree

Redwoods began to linger in the back of Kyros' mind and visions of a massive tree persisted throughout his trip inland. He wasn't sure if the tree was real, fantasy, a glimpse of the past or a premonition.

When he awoke on his first morning back in Arcata, Kyros sat on the fringe of recollection trying to reconstitute the images from his dream. This wasn't the first, but the fifth time he'd wondered near the base of a gargantuan redwood vividly and lucidly.

He thought aloud, "If the tree is real, there has to be a park ranger that would know about it…"

It didn't seem likely they would reveal undisclosed specimens and their locations, yet Kyros speculated he could manage to give a detailed enough description to favor an inciteful one on one conversation.

In the ranger station, Kyros approached the information counter and said, "Hey, my name is Kyros and I was curious if you knew about a specific tree that I am looking for."

The gentlemen responded, "I might, can you describe it?"

Kyros looked around the quiet room to make sure no visitors could hear his detailed description of the Coastal Redwood from his dream.

He closed his eyes and shared a handful of pertinent details. Unfortunately, the ranger was unfamiliar with the tree and apologized for not being of any help. Kyros then asked if he had seen the tree along Damnation Creek Trail in Del Norte Coast Redwoods State Park or near the visitor center in Prairie Creek. The ranger shook his head side to side.

Kyros wasn't deterred and decided that he wanted to extensively explore the parks. He figured that he might not find the tree from his dream, but at least see more iconic individuals and groves before heading back to the Midwest.

Over the next two and a half weeks, Kyros hiked daily and ambitiously, often over ten miles at a time. He systematically hiked most park trails, while living off fruit, nuts, peanut butter and jelly sandwiches and granola bars that he got in the nearby towns of Orick, Klamath and Crescent City.

He preferred to explore the parks with as few belongings as possible, carring only a map, compass, a couple snacks and a quart mason jar of water; which he would refill in the abundant tranquil streams.

The size and structure of the canopies in dozens of the trees were enough to inspire a series of fantasy novels. A few trees that were dead at the top revealed a network of growth as dense as the skyscrapers in Manhattan.

From Prairie Creek, a three-day expedition up Redwood Creek and back down shattered all expectations on how tall trees could be. He couldn't measure but felt confident that the trees were taller than any he had yet witnessed.

His next destination was Jedidiah Smith State Park. While he came across large trees, the park didn't impact him as did the other parks. In fact, it was the Smith River that allured him more than the trees. Stout Grove was breathtaking and beautiful, but the turquoise and emerald waters and tributaries were enchanting and mesmerizing. The river snaked through a steep canyon lined with picturesque forests. The longest fork had to be less than a hundred miles from source to delta, but the force of the water rivaled longer rivers in the Colorado Rockies. Almost the entire watershed spanned across one of the most pristine temperate rainforests on earth. Over a hundred inches of rain a year would fall across steep mountains. Locals told him stories of waterfalls around every bend of the highway and weekly rains with ten inches or more in the height of the winter season.

What did stand out about the forests were the different species of plants. He didn't know, but the Smith River Canyon alone contained numerous species endemic to the region, most of which only grew on the serpentine soil formed from the breakdown of serpentine rock – the same serpentine rock that was in the altar of Joel's family's home.

Occasionally Kyros would come across an exceptionally large redwood, but it wasn't until exploring an unfamiliar part of the park on his last day up north that he became convinced that Jedidiah Smith possessed some extraordinarily large trees. Trees that rivaled even the biggest that he had seen in Prairie Creek less than two weeks before and were as big as the one in his dream. In fact, the third one that caught his attention looked like it could be the exact tree.

He couldn't believe his eyes. Kyros got teary and sat on a log about fifteen feet from the trunk. Time in the grove stopped, while the whole universe kept moving. The tree was so mighty that Kyros couldn't bring himself to trample the plants and soil near her base. Twenty minutes, two hours, it hardly mattered. There was nowhere he needed to be and nothing could distract him from the grandeur and splendor.

An older lady from Belgium was startled when Kyros walked past the second tree. She had been meditating and found this life changing landscape by chance. Despite an obvious language barrier, Kyros could hear her saying that she thought it was special.

The two continued together, sharing impressions of the experience to the best of their abilities. When they came to a giant tree, that was also the first that either encountered in the area, two strangers spanning origins and demographics shared a perfect moment. The sight, as the sun set, was pure bliss. Not even a bird could be heard. The forest was completely silent, and they were in the presence of a tree easily exceeding a thousand years old. A bonded Grandmother and her Grandson would've stood in as much silence. Nothing needed to be said. The tree said it all. Both were able to listen. Both didn't want to miss a second. The countless leaves gently shifted in the breeze.

Near the trailhead, the lady stopped with each hand on a redwood on opposite sides of the path. She spoke hesitantly. Kyros turned around and wasn't sure if she was trying to accurately emphasize a certain point in her third language, English, or if she was bracing herself from judgement. Words came slow, then steadier. "When I walked first, these were almost like portal. You go through the portal and enter into sacred." Her voice and body language were gentle.

Kyros walked up to the trees and placed a hand on each and faced into the amazing grove. As the lady noted, it did look and feel like a gateway into a sacred realm. He felt the energy from the trees exchange between a another as well as him. The lady placed both her hands on the trees once more and said, "They are powerful and are together like brother and sister or brother and brother." She was absolutely right. The two of them, as well as the two trees were resonating in unison and harmony.

Kyros withdrew his hands and took a few steps into the sacred. He felt a little goofy, but he absolutely felt it. Unignorable energies pulsed through himself from the two trees. He felt like he was in a sacred space on the other side of the portal, yet when returning through the gate, the forest noticeably felt less special. Still old growth, but the

Jacob Yastrow

trees were smaller and the landscape seemed off and different.

The lady happened to be driving to Arcata that evening and gave Kyros a ride to the plaza downtown. They drove closer to his camp and he returned to the car with all his belongings in less than five minutes. He got out with only thirty dollars and some change to his name.

In Humboldt Redwoods State Park, Kyros walked the Avenue of the Giants and up the Bull Creek watershed to some of the tallest trees in the world. The trees didn't have the girth of those further north, but they were still huge.

After seeing what was thought to be the most impressive redwood groves and individual trees, Kyros stood on the side of U.S. Highway 101 with his finger out. The next night he had a bus ticket away from the edge of the world. No one was interested in stopping.

He walked along the freeway for about fifteen minutes before nature called. He set his pack on the side of the

road and climbed down the hill to relieve himself. He
pulled up his pants and turned around to see what he
believed to be the biggest tree that he had ever seen. It
reminded him of the tree from the dream. The tree was
blanketed in moss on the south side and the first branch
was over a hundred and fifty feet up. The top was nowhere
in sight. While there were select trees that were bigger, this
was one that had slipped passed the radar. This was the
biggest tree that Kyros had ever seen. In fact, it was the
exact tree from his dream.

Jacob Yastrow

Leaving Humboldt

Before departing the West Coast, Kyros noticed a tree in town for the first time. It easily doubled the height of the five-story building nearby and low and behold it was a redwood. He approached and got excited to see the first branch was only about twelve feet up, which was relatively close to the ground by Coastal Redwood standards. He stashed his backpack in a bush and approached the tree. The bark was spongy. He looked up the trunk, got a good hold, wedged his foot into a deep furrow and thrust himself toward the branch. Using all his strength, he pulled his body up with his right hand high enough to grab the next with his left. He made it. He looked down at the twenty-foot drop and up at the seemingly never-ending staircase of branches. It was the easiest tree he'd ever climbed once that second branch was reached, but the first one was a gamble.

Kyros climbed higher and lost orientation as to which side of the tree he was on. When he got near the top, the branches became too thin to climb any higher. He sat down and reflected on all the time spent in California, but particularly the redwood forests of Humboldt and Del Norte counties. The breeze picked up and he was higher than he'd been in any other tree. He must have rocked four or five feet. Clinging to the branch, he smoked a joint till he grew paranoid. He retreated about fifteen feet down and tried to focus on his breathing. He looked out and realized that he was sitting amongst giants.

The town sat so far below and the only thing as tall as him were the tops of the other redwoods. The wind blew harder and Kyros' smile grew. He wasn't ready to leave this tree. He had another hour till he had to be at the bus station, and he was going to sit in that tree till the last minute. He lit one more joint and thought about the endless possibilities of places to travel. He pulled out his phone and wrote a poem.

There are so many things to see; too many for a lifetime.

There are too many things to learn; go from what others have.

There are so many lives to live; which one is you?

I know the only thing that defines me is whatever it is I be.

There are so many dreams to have; driving us to do what we do.

Some don't stay around long; others permanently persist.

I know the best dreams to have are the ones thought honest and true.

I refuse to chase dreams that others assign to me.

There are so many paths to take; some of them will break you.

Some of them will be hard; others won't make sense.

It may seem like the whole world is against you; too many things getting you down.

At least you will know you stayed true; never strayed far from your heart – now have you?

Jacob Yastrow

He hummed the poem on the down climb and all the way to the bus station. He closed his eyes. Next stop was San Francisco.

The last old growth the bus passed was Richardson Grove State Park. The redwoods were so big that the bus nearly scraped the trunk of a behemoth growing into the road. Kyros said goodbye to the redwoods and grew excited to explore the city. He had the entire evening to wander before the train to Denver would leave the following morning.

He dozed off and was quickly displeased upon waking. The bus was now completely full and out of the forested mountains. He grew uncomfortable and claustrophobic. He wanted out. Panic took over when the bus stopped. It had never happened before, but he couldn't handle the city. There was way too much noise, pollution, traffic, people and commotion for Kyros to tolerate. He b-lined it to the station and managed to get a ticket for a train that was about to depart.

The forest turned to desert, to salt flats, to mountains to plains.

Jacob Yastrow

Moving Forward

The transition back home was unsettling and Kyros began to feel less full by the day. Disconnected to the melodies of the land, his soul struck a deep and dissonant chord on the forty plus hour train trip from San Francisco. Even though it was early fall, and all the trees were still green, the plains felt like tundra compared to the lush rainforests to the west. Three days came and went since his last glimpse of a redwood or the ocean. He was no longer on the edge of the continent.

Kyros needed to connect. In the city, the natural areas weren't impressive. Lights filled the night. Traffic and trash couldn't be ignored. He thought about Maya Bonita Creek, the river, lake and the pond all filled with trash and tragedy. There was only one place to go. Palo answered in the middle of the fourth ring.

"Kyros! How's the journey treating you? Where are you at these days?"

The young man had his spirits lifted just by hearing Palo's voice and experiencing his energy. "Pretty good, man. I went out to Humboldt and explored the redwoods and I just got back into town last night."

Palo responded, "That's wonderful to hear! What did you think? They're pretty unbelievable. They make you feel small, like looking into an unpolluted sky on the new moon."

"I spent three weeks without leaving the old growth and I still can't get over the trees. So impressive. I know I'm going to go back at some point. I feel if every human on earth spent a week in an old growth redwood forest, they would have a lot more respect for the land. Maybe they would all want to get their paper and pulp products from hemp instead of trees."

A man on the long journey across the west sat by Kyros and spent hours explaining the worlds of opportunity that exist for hemp alone. Kyros learned about medicine, fiber, building material, hempcrete, animal bedding, mulch and countless other uses. This traveler had also shared that there was a significant increase in usable material per acre that can be grown in less than a year with hemp, compared to upwards of eighty years or more in a forest of trees.

Kyros' attention returned to the conversation with Palo and he added, "I think hemp is the future. Just think, what if we grew it on just ten percent of the land that is subsidized for growing corn?"

"Absolutely! Words of wisdom right there, my friend. Well, what are you up to today? Do you want to come by for a visit?"

Kyros let out a sigh of relief. "Yes! That is exactly what I need. I miss the land and know the food forest is the only place that I can connect anywhere near as close to nature as I did in the redwoods. Can I come by in fifteen minutes?"

Fourteen minutes later the young man stepped out of the car and was greeted by Joel. The two hugged and headed inside. Joel said, "My mom is giving my dad a brief consultation, but they don't mind if you come in and make yourself comfortable. They will be done soon."

Joel opened the front door and the two quietly walked in. Both parents smiled and returned to their session. Kyros approached the fireplace to gift a redwood cone to the serpentine rock from the Smith River Canyon. The rock guided him. The redwoods had been with him since the greenhouse with Garrett on his second trip to the food forest. Less than a year earlier, the serpentine rock and the notebook with the trees were just sneak peeks into the unimaginable. He looked around and couldn't find the green stone. He stepped away from the hearth and was pleased to see the rock directly in front of his heart. The cone was placed with a folded note.

It read:

Once in a home of people I know
Some friends, some not so much so

I arrived at this new destination in a world of many strangers

In a parking lot, a National Park or town

It all begins with a smile or 'hello'

A beauty arises from a gesture so simple

It doesn't take long for one to realize they've stumbled

upon such exceptionally extraordinary beings

We attract what we put out

Honing in like a hound

A sixth sense that I'm not always cognizant about

Now in a place far from where I started sits a limbo between

stranger and friend

You can tell when you've stumbled into an honestly great

thing when it is so difficult to leave

Once in a home of people I know

Some friends, some not so much so

Now in a place far from where I started

We are hardly strangers, but friends.

He walked over to the sink and filled up a glass of water. Joel had mentioned that his father was getting a consultation, but Kyros didn't know what that entailed.

The mother investigated Palo's mouth and inspected the top and underside of his tongue. Then, she moved his left arm a little closer onto the table and turned it so his elbow was facing down. Three fingers were placed on the wrist, each spaced slightly apart. She closed her eyes and breathed gently. After feeling his left wrist, the same was done to his right.

The words for Palo were too quiet to be made out by Kyros on the other side of the home.

"What were you doing?" Kyros politely asked once they all exchanged greetings and sentiments.
She smiled and said, "I was listening to his pulse and reading his tongue."
"For what?" Kyros hoped that his quick response didn't seem rude.

The mother was unfazed. "Here, sit down." She directed him to a chair and kneeled in front of him. She oriented his

176

left elbow onto his left knee and spaced her index, middle and ring finger on his wrist. "By the nature of the pulse I gain insight to your health and constitution at this moment of existence. I check both wrists, because our bodies are natural representations of the world. Within the world the duality of yin and yang exists together, balancing and defining the other." She spoke of the same duality that Palo introduced him to on his first visit to the food forest.

"The pulse in one arm lets me feel your yin energies and the other lets me feel your yang energies. Your tongue is also a blueprint for the health of the body. Like a map, different regions of the tongue have corresponding locations to specific internal organs. Will you open your mouth?" She shared, while pointing to different parts of his tongue. Kyros held a pocket mirror from her purse so he could see exactly where she was pointing. "This part is your stomach, this part your spleen, and your heart is over here. Your liver and gallbladder are here, and the lungs are right there." Kyros handed her the mirror and closed his mouth.

She continued answering his question, "Your tongue gives me a visual aid of the health and state of each organ. This includes the moisture and heat levels within your body. I can gain insight as to whether you are hot, cold, wet or dry.

"Tongue and pulse reading are ancient forms of medicine that predate history in the Western World. By understanding the constitution of the body, organs and organ systems over short and long periods for each individual, medical practitioners would be able to suggest and apply specific herbs and remedies that wouldn't aggravate individual constitutions. For instance, if your body is already cool and damp, I'm not likely going to give you something cooling and damp, but if your body is warm, a cooling herb might be a better remedy for you as an individual."

"Wow that is amazing! Where did you learn all of that?"

"There are individuals all over the world who maintain the knowledge and traditions of the past. They teach in a way that respects the plants and the people who kept the teachings of the plants alive. I have studied in Arizona, the

Pacific Northwest, to the remote mountains of China, India, as well as from the shamans in South America that work with sacred Ayahuasca plants. However, some of the greatest knowledge about the plants came from the plants themselves. They taught me."

The mother had to tend to her plants. She said her goodbyes and headed out the door with her basket, some clippers and a small jar of tobacco. Joel had gone to muck out a few stalls in the barn.

Palo and Kyros sat at the table and ate fresh peaches that were picked that morning. They each exchanged experiences and lessons learned over the last several months. When it came time for Kyros to go home for dinner, Palo shared the keys to the next step in Kyros' journey.

Palo inquired, "What is your plan now?"

Kyros looked at his hands and fiddled with his thumbs. "That's the thing. I just don't know. I would love to work with you guys for the next few months until winter. I could save up some money and not have to pay for produce or meat. I think that my mom would let me stay with my family if I was working with you at least part time."

"Well, that's a start. You know you're always welcome to work for food. I can't pay you much, but how about this? What if I pay you eight dollars an hour under the table, but you can take all the produce you can eat, some squash to store for the winter, eggs as needed and I'll give you and your family a few pounds of meat a week. I'll even let you take first pick at the jack-o-lantern pumpkins if that's what you're into." They both chuckled.

"That's a good enough deal that I think my parents will let me use their extra car! I would love that. Can I start in a week?"

"That sounds great to me." Palo shook Kyros' hand and the two of them hugged. They were family indeed. "Kyros, I do want you to listen to your heart. If the wind is guiding you to do something, you need to take it seriously. Even if it seems reckless or impulsive, you still need to do it if it will make your heart sing. You will be guided to your highest path. You are light. You can be light. Be a light for yourself and it will help others be a light in themselves."

Kyros thanked Palo and headed to dinner. With a few minutes to spare in the parking lot, Kyros wrote a poem. He was truly inspired by Palo and yearned to be half as inspiring as the tender of the food forest.

Divinity within me

Like you, I am light

A honing in on my heart

Nurturing my intentions

Doing completely

The path not guided by fear

Very simple at its core

It is our nature

Society chains us blind

Free your mind from illusions

Let your heart guide you

Tune in to your highest path

The mind, a humble servant

A priceless jewel

Freed when guided by the heart

Allow the mind time to roam

Give it time to speak

Don't become deceived by it

Make decisions out of love

It's the only way

You will help the many glow

Show the dim to shine brightly

You don't need to try

Live fully within the self

A model or a blueprint

Be an example

Autonomous, not asleep

You know what is best for you

Each of them do too

Their hearts aren't yet attuned

Words and actions, planted seeds

Every one won't sprout

Yet, a forest will still grow

Jacob Yastrow

Maya Bonita Cleanup

The following morning, one of Kyros' first thoughts was to go revive the polluted natural area that had haunted him for too long. A breakfast burrito to-go was prepared and he drove off down the highway. He was surprised by how different the landscape looked and how much the forest had filled in around the massive stumps in about a year. By midafternoon Kyros had filled ten trash bags and consolidated an equal amount in a pile. The creek was almost completely free of trash, but he was going to need help to clean the lake and pond.

He went out on a limb and drove into the lot that to his relief was still abandoned. By the river, Bacchus Sophos came into view. Nearby was Green Desert. Kyros greeted his friends and turned to Green. "We have to clean up the natural area a few miles down the highway. I cleaned the creek, but the pond and lake are a mess! There are appliances, tires and everything else you could think of. We could probably do it in a day, but we'd need at least a dozen people. Maybe some dollies and a trailer."

Green and Bacchus were both happy to help and thought they could round up at least a couple more volunteers in the next day or two. They planned to meet in the same place in two mornings about an hour after sunrise and do as much as possible with the people that showed up.

Kyros' parents and sister weren't pleased that the rendezvous point was in the parking lot with all the homeless people and he tried to assure them not to worry. Turnout was a success. Green had got the cleanup approved to be the senior class project for his students. They couldn't get a bus on such short notice, but the class had piled into three large vans and was on their way to mile post two hundred-sixty-two.

Kyros started walking toward the group of people and his mom snapped. She yelled, "Do not go walking into that group of people. It isn't safe." Several homeless men and women turned their heads at the flustered mom chasing after her son.

"Mom, it's fine. I just gotta grab Bacchus; I told him we'd give him a ride."

"You want to give him a ride? I am not going to let a dirty bum into my car." Several others turned and others were waking up in disgust that they were being bothered before eight in the morning by a hysterical lady.

Kyros found Bacchus just in time. Bacchus looked at Kyros' mom and said, "I understand your feelings, but I assure you I have only the best intentions to help your son clean the natural area. I don't want anything from you other than your understanding. If you don't want me to ride with you I won't, but your generosity would be much appreciated. Your son is an amazing man and I can tell that you did an outstanding job raising him. Please, at least give me a chance to sway your opinions about me." Bacchus opened the driver door for her with a grin.

Kyros watched the same man that changed his tire and his perspective begin to change his mom's perspective. The parking lot was tense, and the situation was only seconds from escalating out of hand, and now this "bum" was getting in his mom's car with his family. Even Kyros' dad gave Bacchus an approving head nod and fist bump as he slid into the middle seat to make room.

Kyros was so impressed but for some reason not surprised. He knew that such honest and pure intentions could be felt between very different people and that Bacchus' authenticity shed no doubt.

Everyone grabbed ropes, trash bags, gloves, rubber boots and waders. The group fell silent as the ground leveled and they saw the open area. Kyros watched their facial expressions, remembering his feelings the first time witnessing the atrocity. Instantaneously, everyone was more compelled to clean the trash. Some whispered about the stumps. Others murmured about the smells.

Planao, Zeus, Apollo and Demeter walked up the hill. Kyros watched his parents process their son hugging these strange looking, dirty, homeless humans and he could only smile. He was thrilled that Bacchus got his friends to join and it was quite the surprise.

Students, parents and homeless began working together. Some people were picking up trash and others were in the water, tying ropes around larger items to hoist onto shore. Many were carrying trash down the hill, loading it onto a long trailer to take to the dump. A group of older ladies from the community showed up and started cutting-back trails that made it easier for everyone to access the lake.

The area started to look significantly better fast and most of the people were now cleaning trash and debris from the forest and away from the lake. It hadn't even been six hours, yet the group turned the dump into a very beautiful and pleasant place. It still smelled a little, but the water was flowing and everything that smelled was out of the water. A brave volunteer carried two dead beavers a few hundred feet from the shore and buried them.

Jacob Yastrow

Kyros was so impressed and felt an immense sense of bliss to see the progress made. The dirty and polluted natural area haunted him for over a year and he made that special piece of land better with the help of friends, family and many strangers.

A poem had been at work in his mind. He had been reciting verses while he worked that day. The man looked around and was pleased to see his parents talking to his transient and eclectic friends. Even the older ladies were laughing and enjoying themselves to the company. Nobody was displeased by the presence of five haggard recluses within arms-reach. Kyros took several minutes to write while the group of people chatted amongst themselves.

The land is my meditation
It brings me peace
Reground after the city
Land beneath bare feet

The forest is my meditation

Reminding me to breathe

Helps me forget about the people and focus on the trees

The birds are my meditation

Bringing these parts songs

Loud enough to silence the city

Quiet enough to hear my thoughts

The river is my meditation

Its currents calm my mind

The water, too, on a journey

To see sister in New Orleans

An older lady approached Kyros and he put his phone in his pocket while standing up from the log. She grabbed his right hand between both of her hands. Her pale, wrinkled skin was dry and soft. "Are you the young man that coordinated this clean up?"

Kyros smiled ear to ear. "I am. Thank you so much for helping. It means so much to me. I first came here a year ago and I was appalled by the neglect. I started to cry when I saw all of the pollution and dead fish."

The woman sniffled and used her hand to wipe a tear from her cheek. She placed her right hand on his shoulder. "When I was a little girl, I happened to venture from the road up the creek. It became my safe place. I would run away from the world and retreat to the riverbank where I would play with the plants and animals. I was never lonely. Over time my connection grew.

"The owl started to remain perched in the cottonwoods, even when I splashed in the shallows. Osprey, hawks and eagles began to dive into the water to feast with no concern for me, the ten-year-old girl in heaven. Deer warmed up enough to stay grazing as long as I kept my distance and respect for them. A squirrel would chew holes in my lunch sack and eat whatever he could get his little hands on. I remember the first time I had an avocado and that frickin' rascal ate the half that I saved for later.

"I would wander for hours, sometimes coming home after dark. I didn't want to tell my parents of my joys in the woods. I was scared people would ruin it, just like everything else. For years I kept this place a secret. I talked about the beauty of nature with only nature. Even the way the beaver scared me when he smacked his tail too loud or swam too close. I was mesmerized, not just by the ability of the beaver to eat through entire cottonwood trunks, but also in the ability of the tree to remain standing after being half eaten."

Kyros thought about the redwoods and the massive caverns burned almost entirely through their trunks.

Elaine continued, "One day, my dad silently followed me into the woods to see where his daughter spent hours at a time. I had seen the full beauty of nature and I was part of the beauty. My dad saw deer and that meant hunting.

"My dad went out and told all his friends of his "honey hole," and they built a stand in my favorite tree. At first, my dad was okay with the way I spent my time in the forest and meadow, but before long, three more stands were built.

Afterwards, my dad wouldn't even let me go there to visit the plants and animals. I was banished from my home.

"One night, I grabbed a lantern and walked back to the place I hadn't seen for over a year. My flower friends had been trampled and trash was strewn around the trunks of all four trees with stands. Trash was in the water. There were no more deer. No more owls. No more moss on the ground.

"Several months later, a hunter dropped his lantern while setting up early Christmas Morning. The understory was dormant and since it was an unusually dry year, the forest went up in flames. It all burned that morning. The flames were extinguished by the first snow of the winter on the morning of January 1st.

"The area was never the same and had since been neglected land that the county didn't know what to do with. But you…" Elaine pointed right at Kyros, "…you cleaned up the trash from over fifty years of neglect."

Kyros started to experience a similar resonating vibration to that which he felt with Palo on his first visit to the food forest the previous year. Also, the same feeling from when his hands were on both trees in the gateway to the sacred forest with the Belgian lady. It was only the third time, nevertheless the feeling was unmistakable. Elaine's words hit him like a train. The man started crying and fell to his knees. Between the sobs and gasps he managed to ask, "Why did no one clean it up?"

The lady hunched over a little more. "No one cared. I asked everyone I knew and they all laughed. I pleaded and begged, but it was dismissed. No one would hear me. No one could see me. I would try and fill my basket with trash, but it wasn't safe. Things were sharp and rusty and had weird smells. I accepted defeat and went on with my life.

"Right now, for the first time since my dad saw the deer, this oasis is starting to feel home again." She knelt down to her knees, crying and hugging Kyros as tight as a mother. These tears weren't those of grief, but pure joy and elation.

Kyros and Elaine cried together. While Elaine couldn't do as much of the cleanup as Kyros, and despite the fact that they were over forty years in age apart, they were equals. It didn't need to be communicated nor confirmed, and they both knew it as truth.

A beautiful butterfly flew by and disappeared into the forest. Kyros hadn't just learned how to see, he was ready to fly.

Made in the USA
Monee, IL
29 May 2021

69055764R10115